Murder at the Knitting Retreat

GLENDA BARNETT

Copyright © 2022 by Glenda Barnett

All rights reserved.

No part of this book may be reproduced in any form or by any electronic or mechanical means, including information storage and retrieval systems, without written permission from the author, except for the use of brief quotations in a book review.

Books by the Author

The St Urith With Well Series:

The Curious Curiosity

Celia Finds An Angel

The Unfurled Moth

Wedding Fever

Short Stories - Little Red & other stories

For
Peter and Simon

"My greatest comfort and relief is in the consolation of friends"
St Augustine

Constructive Knitting

A silver blue open top sports car overtook her taxi. As it passed, the good looking driver gave May a cheeky wink. In a good holiday mood, she couldn't help but smile. She leaned back on the seat and closed her eyes, thinking about the week ahead. She was so looking forward to relaxing with good food, a beautiful room and lovely gardens set in a luxury hotel. The icing on the cake was that this holiday was a knitting retreat and there would be a workshop every day. She could knit already but these workshops were to teach you how to knit socks and she was really looking forward to it. She had tried to knit them before but had given up. She was determined to crack the skill this week as she planned to knit all her family and friends socks for Christmas presents. It was also time away that she so badly needed, from family, work, even her best friend Trudy. She loved Trudy. They had been friends forever but she needed a break from her constantly trying to set her up with her fiance's friends, work colleagues, even her Amazon delivery guy who Trudy thought was cute. It had been six months since she broke up with her longtime boyfriend Eddie and she was finally beginning to feel like her old self. The last thing she wanted was another man expecting her to change who she was just to fit into his idea of what a woman should be. At this sock knitting retreat there probably wouldn't be any men and she wouldn't know anyone anyway and more importantly they wouldn't know her or anything about her humiliating break-up. She wouldn't have to speak or hear his name all week. Hallelujah.

Arrival & False Assumptions

As her taxi pulled up they were just in time to see the gates close on the silver blue sports car that had overtaken them half a mile back. May told the driver to drop her off here and she would walk the rest of the way. She pulled up the handle of her suitcase and, with a little wave to the taxi driver, turned to the large green imposing gates in front of her, excitement blooming in her stomach. A stone wall ran either side of the gates enclosing the wealth trees and garden and she could see no sign of the house. Looking around she found a bell above a speaker set in one of the pillars and pushed it. Something unintelligible quacked at her from the speaker.

"Sorry, I didn't get that, can you say again?"

A second stream of gobbledygook emitted from the speaker, equally unintelligible to May.

"I'm sorry, I can't understand what you are saying. I'm here for the knitting retreat, can you let me in?"

The speaker burst into sound again at the same time as a second taxi pulled up. The driver hopped out, opened his boot and hauled out two suitcases as two silver-haired women climbed out from the back, chattering away like a pair of sparrows. The taxi pulled away with a squeal of wheelspin, sending gravel flying up and one of the women to remark,

"He thinks he's Starsky and Hutch."

"I didn't like Starsky and Hutch. Which one?" asked the second woman.

"Which one what?"

"Well, Starsky or Hutch?"

"I don't know, it was only an expression. I don't know which one is which."

"Which one did he look like?"

"I don't know which one he looked like," the first woman now sounded frustrated.

"Why did you say he did then?" persisted the second woman. "You should say what you mean. She turned, pinched her lips together and huffed. Unfortunately, she then caught sight of May.

"You! Don't just stand there gawping, take our cases and open those gates, I'm desperate for a cup of tea."

The first woman put her hand on the other's arm and started to speak, "Josie, I don't think...."

"Oh stop wittering Mary." They both stopped close to the gates and the first woman looked at May expectedly.

The speaker spewed a further stream of nonsense and the gates slowly opened. May pushed the shoulder strap of her bag further up her shoulder, grabbed the handle of her suitcase and walked through. She knew she was being childish and rude by ignoring the woman but the woman had been rude first. After the way her boyfriend had treated her she had decided she wasn't going to accept crap from anybody. Especially not here where she had come to relax, unwind and enjoy herself without thinking about him.

"Excuse me! Hey you, what about our cases?"

"I think we have to take them ourselves Josie, I don't think she works here."

Josie sniffed, "then why didn't she say so then? Come along Mary, don't dawdle."

May had silently listened to this pantomime but carried on up the winding drive, with its high hedge bordering either side. Note to self, steer clear of those two, she thought. She could hear them still twittering away, please knitting Gods let there be at least a couple of other women that she could talk to over the next week or it was going to be a very long one.

May could feel the rise of the drive in her calves as she walked, her suitcase bouncing over the many potholes. If she blocked out the chattering pair who were now quite a way behind her, all she could hear was the birds. The scent from the honeysuckle tickled her nose as the hedges on the right hand side gave way to a large vegetable garden and cut flower beds with a row of greenhouses. It felt as if she had been walking for ages when she rounded a sharp bend and the lane sloped down to a large courtyard with stone buildings off to the right and what appeared to be the back of the house on the left. The house was built out of stone and was originally a hunting and fishing lodge. It was an absolute gem, set in the most beautiful gardens. Some lodge May thought as she admired the turrets on each end and made her way to the arched door set in the middle.

The Welcome

May opened the door and dragged her suitcase over the threshold and made her way to a tall desk set back in the hallway. It was quite dark but the oak panelled walls hung with pictures making it feel cosy and welcoming. There wasn't anybody behind the desk but a shiny bell sat waiting to be rung. May was still waiting for someone to come when the two women caught up and entered the door behind her.

"Still waiting? Ring the bell Mary." Josie ordered.

Mary shook the bell vigorously.

An elegant woman in her early fifties appeared, tall, slim, her honey-blonde hair in a neat chignon, wearing a dark green silk shirt and tailored black trousers.

"Ok, that's enough, you will give us all a headache. Now who was first?" She asked.

"Josie Harris and this is my sister Mary Beal. I hope you have given us the best rooms, I booked early to ensure you would.

Mary looked at May apologetically and mouthed sorry, May shrugged her shoulders and raised an eyebrow.

"Welcome to Merton Manor, my name is Ursula Jeffries, we hope you enjoy your stay. Jazz will take you to your rooms and sherry will be served at 12.30 on the patio prior to lunch.

A young woman appeared and Mrs Jeffries addressed her handing over the keys.

"Take these ladies up to rooms 216 and 217 Jazz, please."

Jazz walked to the end of the hall, "follow me ladies."

"You don't expect me to carry my own suitcase! What sort of establishment is this?" Josie tapped her toe on the parquet flooring, arms folded.

"Jazz, would you mind?" Mrs Jeffries asked apologetically.

Jazz, face like thunder, walked back and snatched up the handle of the suitcase, muttering under her breath, "what did your last servant die of?"

Mary heard the remark and flushed but Josie chose to ignore it and with a nod to Mrs Jeffries, followed Jazz.

May turned to the desk and smiled. "Hello I'm May Wood, I'm expecting all your rooms to be the best."

Ursula Jeffries barely cracked a frosty smile, "I believe the room will be to your satisfaction." She turned the register around for May to sign, then passed a key over "219, I am sure you can manage your own suitcase, just follow the others."

May walked in the direction the other guests had taken until she came to a second large hallway with an imposing flight of stairs. A beautiful display of garden flowers rested on a mahogany side table, their colours reflected in the polished surface. A large oak door was obviously the front door. She started up the stairs, bumping her suitcase up each step. When she arrived at the top there was a long galleried landing, paintings covered the walls and small table and glass cases displayed objet d'art, plenty to explore and discover later. She rested her hands on the mahogany balustrade and leaned over looking down to the hall below. A hand came down on top of hers making her jump.

"Not thinking of jumping are we? The place is bad but not that bad."

"Faggots and gin! You gave me a fright." May said, snatching her hand away and stepping back to see who this was. She took him in, early thirties, artfully tousled hair that must have taken ages to perfect, a pair of piercing blue eyes set off by his tan and a cynical smile.

"No, I was just getting my bearings."

He turned and leaned back on the balustrade so that he was facing her. "Are you lost? I'd be very happy to show you the way. In fact I would be very happy to take you anyway."

May looked at him. Really? Cheesy or what? Who was this creep? I've only been here five minutes, is there something about me that attracts these losers? He wore a soft pale blue linen shirt opened too far at the neck, revealing a toned chest and a very tight pair of black trousers. You've got player written all over you mate and I'm not about to be your latest conquest.

"That's very kind of you but I'm a grown up, I think I can manage to find my own way." She turned and walked along the landing checking door numbers as she went. She fought the urge to look back over her shoulder but couldn't resist, unfortunately he was watching and smiled smugly before giving her a nod and heading back down the stairs.

Faggots! I wonder who he is and if he is staying here or lives here? The latter I suspect I can't see him sitting knitting socks.

The Perfect Room

May soon found her room and was pleasantly surprised to find it was more like a bedroom in a private home than a hotel. It was bright and fresh, the bird-themed wallpaper was obviously hand painted and the chairs were upholstered in a pretty floral fabric. The bed was huge and covered in a white-work counterpane with many squishy cushions. May opened the door to the en-suite bathroom and discovered to her delight a giant roll-top bath positioned next to the window with views over the gardens. She stretched her arms out wide and spun around. Oh yes, this is just what I needed, a bit of spoiling in luxurious surroundings. She unpacked her suitcase, hanging her clothes in a wardrobe that was almost the same size as the kitchen in her flat, truly a 'Narnia' wardrobe. She laid out her toiletries in the bathroom and her other bits and pieces on the antique dressing table in the room then threw herself backwards onto the bed, stretching her arms wide.

Memories

As she lay there, her thoughts went back to the last few months and the conversations that she'd had with her best friend Trudy. It was the beginning of the end for her long term relationship. She had been with Eddie for three years and thought that he was 'the one' as the magazines are always saying but the relationship didn't seem to be going anywhere. Trudy said he needed a few nudges. She said that men are happy with the status quo and will trundle along forever unless nudged in the right direction. She said her Kai was quite happy bouncing from his mum's house to her flat. He didn't need to grow up as he was getting his washing done and dinner at his mum's and sex at hers then out to five-a-side on a Friday night and drinks after with the lads.

But May protested, "didn't he propose to you on a romantic night out?"

Trudy explained that he did but only after she'd had a secret meeting with his mum.

"Go on."

"Well, she was fed up with looking after him, after all he was a grown man. She wanted to move on with her own life and my biological clock was on fast forward so we hatched a plan. She told him he had three months to find somewhere else to live as she was going back to college to study viticulture and oenology and she had rented his room out to a fellow student called Tim. He couldn't move into mine as there wasn't room in my cupboard to squeeze in a double bed and anyway he hated Davey my flatmate coz he's always walking around in his boxers and six pack on show and it makes him feel inadequate."

"He never said that?"

"No, but he always pulls his tummy in and tries to push his chest out. So this night, we were getting down to it on the sofa when Davey comes in straight from the gym. Strips of his tee-shirt as he walks in the room, all tanned muscles with a sheen of sweat, lycra gym shorts leaving nothing to the imagination and plonks himself down in the armchair one leg over the arm, everything on display and starts to chat. I mean I'm used to it but I still enjoy the view. Kai was evil and frustrated, I whispered in his ear 'if only we had our own place we'd never be disturbed.' He proposed a week later."

"Eddie doesn't live with his mum, he already has his own place, it's me who lives at home, so that won't work."

"Yes but May you have never ever even been to Eddie's place. You either meet out somewhere or go back to yours."

"I know, you're right, but that's only because Eddie likes his own space and he's told me his place is really very small and he has been so busy working he hasn't had time to redecorate. When he's had a chance to sort it then I'll be the first visitor. And don't look at me like that."

"Well, I'd have thought three years was long enough to redecorate." Trudy sniffed.

"That's not fair, he's been concentrating on his career."

And then Trudy had come up with her big idea. May groaned as she thought about it.

"I have an idea, why don't you surprise him."

"What do you mean?"

"Buy some paint and brushes, put on a sexy pair of dungarees and rock up to his place ready for action. He will love it."

"Do you really think so?"

"What man wouldn't? Think what fun the two of you will have, you could take a bottle of wine, order in pizza, oh it will be so romantic."

"I don't know Trud"

"Oh come on, May, you're being ridiculous. Don't you think it's weird that you've been in a relationship for three years and you've never set foot in his place? I mean it's a bit strange isn't it?"

"No it's not, he works a lot and gets tired."

I sat up on the bed and looked out of the window, remembering that conversation still hurt. I tried to defend Eddie but Trudy was right. It was strange but he always seemed to have a good reason why we couldn't go back to his. So I agreed to try Trudy's mad idea and that was where my life fell apart. That was ten months ago and I'm getting over it but I needed a change of scene and this knitting retreat was it.

She pushed off the bed and squished her toes in the sheepskin rug. This is the life, she thought. I'm going to forget the past and enjoy this week and be ready to leave here recovered and looking forward to the future. Wishing she had a drink to reinforce the toast she looked around for a mini-bar but there wasn't one. On the dressing table she found a booklet titled 'Sock Knitting Retreat' and was browsing through it when she heard a bell ringing in the distance. Checking the itinerary and her phone she knew it was the bell for lunch. She washed her hands in the basin and ran a few drops of water through her hair, running her fingers through to give it a lift. Locking the door behind her she headed down to find lunch and meet her fellow guests.

On The Terrace - Making New Friends

Lunch had been set out on white wrought iron tables on the terrace with its views over the lawns down to the river Heddon which flowed from the edges of Exmoor to the North Devon coast at Heddon's Mouth. The tables were already laid with a cloth, china and cutlery, glasses and a jug of water with ice and lemon. The parasols were up and people were already seated at various tables around the patio. She realised she was the last to arrive and hesitated for a moment as to where to sit.

"Cooee! Over here," A tall attractive man with a shaved head sporting a gold earring was beckoning.

May looked around, not sure if he was calling her.

"Yes you sweetie, come on come over and join us,"

He wore a tight turquoise tee-shirt which outlined the shape of two nipple rings and was tucked into tight jeans with a fancy buckled belt. He smiled as he pulled out a chair for her at their table for four and she sat down.

"Thank you, that's kind of you. I'm May."

"You are very welcome Sweetie. I'm Tony, this gorgeous beast is my husband Michael and this charming young lady is Lucy."

"Hi, everyone, are you all here for the knitting retreat?" May asked.

"Yes, but between you and me and the birds , Michael and I can't knit for toffees, except he'll probably be good at it, he's good at everything." Tony put his head back and laughed out loud.

"Silly question but why are you here then?" May asked.

"Well, that's because of me, I needed a break but we didn't want to face the awful summer traffic by going too far and I've always been fascinated with this house and its magical gardens. I can't quite believe I'm actually staying here. " Michael said, squeezing Tony's knee.

"I saw this retreat advertised and booked it straight away as a surprise for him." Tony put his hand on Michaels arm and they smiled at each other. "But I am a bit nervous about the knitting."

"Well, you never know you might find that you are both good at it and apparently sock knitting is addictive. How about you Lucy, do you already knit socks?" May asked.

Lucy, startled to be addressed, looked up shyly. "I don't but I really want to learn."

"Do you knit already?" May asked.

"Oh yes, it keeps me occupied in the evenings."

"Are you like me, have fidgety fingers? I can't sit still and do nothing, I'm either knitting, sewing or reading. I knit mostly in the evenings whilst watching telly."

"We don't have a television, mother didn't like them but now she's gone the evenings are very quiet." Lucy's voice tailed off.

"Oh I'm sorry ducky, did your mother pass recently?" Tony asked.

Lucy's eyes filled with tears as she nodded, "yes, three months ago."

All three of them expressed their condolences and Michael, tears in his own eyes, patted Lucy's hand that rested on the table.

Thankfully, Jazz arrived with their lunch at that moment and everyone was eager to see what was on offer. A cut glass bowl of fresh salad, lettuce, peppers, tomatoes, onions and feta cheese was placed in the middle of the table and bowls of olives, tuna, and a plate of cold meats alongside. Jazz then opened a bottle of Sauvignon Blanc and poured a little into each glass before leaving.

"Wow this looks delicious, it's so good having someone cook for you especially with a glass of cold wine. Now I feel like I'm really on holiday." May said, taking a sip.

"Oh dear, I don't drink, what shall I do?" Lucy had flushed red with embarrassment.

"You don't have to drink it ducky, it's not compulsory but why don't you try it first, see if you like it." Tony said.

"Well I don't know if I should, my mother always said alcohol is the devil's work."

Tony rolled his eyes at May.

Poor little soul thought May, bet her mother was a domineering old hag. "Tony's right, why don't you try a sip with your dinner, it's a good aid for digestion." May said.

"Well if you all think so," Lucy looked at them all in turn and they all nodded. They tried not to stare at her as she raised the glass and took a tiny sip, her eyes popped open and then she took a large gulp which made her eyes water and left her coughing.

They couldn't help but laugh, May patted her back, "You'd better take it easy at first, perhaps put a little water with it."

Lucy smiled, "I think that's a very good idea."

Tony poured some water into everyone's water glass and a little in Lucy's wine glass. Holding his own wine glass up he said, "cheers everyone, here's to a great week."

They all clinked glasses and then tucked into their lunch. When they had finished and the plates had been cleared away, Jazz brought out fat slices of lemon cheesecake for them all and asked if they would like tea or coffee.

"Coffee for me, or I might nod off this afternoon after that delicious lunch," Tony said.

They all had coffee and whilst she was drinking hers, May pushed her chair back and took the opportunity to look at the other guests, who she assumed were also on the knitting retreat.

Who's Who

"Do you want the low-down on the others? Me and Michael have met them all except for the sour-faced woman and her friend." Tony asked, leaning forward conspiratorially.

"Go on then," May grinned, looking at Tony and Michael, these two were going to be a hoot.

"Ursula Jeffries inherited this house from her father, then she married Colonel Jeffries. They don't have children but there is a very deliciously handsome nephew of the Colonel's called Ryder. I've seen pictures of him in celebrity magazines always with a different woman hanging off his arm. He's something in the city but has a room here and likes to bring his friends down for country weekends. We think the Jeffries are a bit short of money and that's why they are starting these retreats because it's always been a private home." Michael said.

"Those two ladies over by the rose arch are Evelyn and Alice from Wales, they go on a lot of retreats but this is the first time they've been here. Over there is Sheila and Hazel. They are best friends from Kent and they also go on a lot of knitting retreats. I don't know the sourpuss and her friend." Tony said, pursing his mouth.

"They are Josie and Mary, they arrived just after me and I heard their names when they checked in. I know I shouldn't say it but one of them is a right old bag, the other one seems okay."

Just then a short slim woman in her fifties appeared in the middle of the terrace. She had a friendly face and her chestnut hair sprinkled with grey lay in a plait over one shoulder and a pair of gold-coloured wire-framed glasses perched on the end of her nose. She tapped a teaspoon against a mug gaining everyone's attention.

Introductions

"Hello everyone, my name is Ivy and I will be your tutor for this week. Aren't we lucky to have this beautiful weather? Can I have a show of hands from those of you who would like to stay out here and hold this afternoon's session in the garden."

All hands went up except Josie's and when she gave Mary a stern look, she lowered her hand.

"Well, that's unanimous. I know I prefer to be outside and this weather is perfect as it's not too hot but let's keep the parasols up we don't want to get too hot to knit.

"Are we really expected to sit out here in this heat?" Josie asked no one in particular with a sniff of disapproval, waving her napkin to and fro in front of her face.

Ivy looked over to Josie, recognising she would be the difficult customer this week but decided to ignore the question. She didn't want to get into an argument and the majority of the guests wanted to stay out here.

"Shall we say ten minutes for a comfort break?"

A few of the guests left the terrace but most remained chatting amongst themselves. When everyone was back apart from Josie, Ivy walked over to a table which was covered over with a linen cloth. As the minutes ticked by the guests started to get restless, eager to start the afternoon workshop.

Tony decided he'd had enough waiting. "Look Ivy, we're all here, it's not fair that we should have to wait for one person. Can we make a start, we've given her long enough, it's nearly twenty minutes?"

"Yes of course. Let's start this afternoon's session by going around and introducing ourselves and tell me what you hope to get out of this week?"

Before she could say anymore Josie arrived. "You had better not have started without me, that would be plain rude. I've paid good money for this and..." Before she could say anymore, Mary stood up and took her arm, trying to placate her.

"Josie, we haven't started, we were waiting for you."

Josie sat down mollified and smug now that she was the centre of attention.

"So shall we all introduce ourselves? I'm sure by the end of your stay we will all be the best of friends." She looked to the table on her right, "would you like to start us off?"

The short plump fair-haired woman, dressed in paisley patterned blue summer trousers and a plain blue tee-shirt spoke. "Hello, my name is Sheila and I come from Kent. I'm fairly new to knitting and I have never tried socks but I really want to learn." She smiled at the group.

Her companion of equal height and wearing a similar outfit but in green spoke next. "I'm Hazel, Sheila's best friend. I also live in Kent. I'm a knitter but I want to learn how to knit socks."

At the next table there were two women wearing almost identical outfits of pink and purple hand-knitted tops and navy trousers. "My name is Evelyn from Welsh Wales and I'm an experienced knitter who needed a break and I've never been to North Devon before."

"I'm Alice, also from Wales and an experienced knitter."

"And what about over here," Ivy looked across at May's table.

"I'm Tony and this is my husband Michael," before he could say anymore they could all hear the word "disgusting!" coming from the last table to speak.

Tony carried on. "Neither of us can knit but we are keen to learn and looking forward to spending time in these beautiful surroundings." As he sat down he reached for Michaels hand.

May went next. "I'm May I love knitting and I was ready for a holiday, this retreat looked ideal especially with the added bonus of learning how to knit socks.

. . .

"My name is Lucy, and I'm from Bristol, I…"

"Speak up can't hear you," interrupted Josie causing Lucy to flush red and look down at the table.

Ivy quickly came to her rescue. "Hi Lucy and lastly would you two like to introduce yourselves?" She asked, looking at Josie and Mary.

"My name is Josie and I am a very experienced knitter so you had better be on your toes young lady. Oh and this is Mary, my sister."

Ivy's heart sank a little, that's all she needed a blooming know-it-all on the course, and one who seemed bigoted and nasty. She desperately needed this course to be successful in the hopes there would be more. Ever since Covid she had been struggling to keep her yarn shop afloat but it wasn't only her livelihood it was her home because she lived in the flat above. She crossed her fingers behind her back and said a little prayer that it would go well.

"Great, well I'm sure we'll all get to know each other over the coming few days." Ivy reached for two corners of the cloth and lifted it off with a flourish. There were oohs and aahs at the gorgeous array of jewel coloured yarns some patterned some plain spread across the table. "I'm very pleased to share with you the joy of knitting socks but I warn you it can be very addictive." There were a few chuckles from her audience and Ivy began to feel more confident.

"Let's talk a little bit about socks. Some of the oldest knitted socks were made in ancient Egypt, so they have been around for a very long time."

"Excuse me young lady. You are wrong." Josie interrupted. "If you're the so-called expert supposed to be teaching us then you should get your facts right."

Ivy flushed and her stomach sunk, oh please let the week not go like this with this woman challenging my every word. I need to establish my position or she'll walk over me. And what's with the derogatory 'young lady' I'm in my fifties for goodness sake. She took a deep breath. "I'm always open to hearing new information, Josie. Would you like to share your knowledge with us?"

Josie stood up, preened, enjoying being the centre of attention, Her sister sitting next to her looked embarrassed. "This is fact! The first knitted garments were made in Jutland in 1500 BC." Jocie said with a smug smile on her face.

"But were they socks?" asked May, annoyed at Josie for interrupting.

"Excuse me?" Josie said.

"Those first knitted garments, were they socks?" May persisted.

"Does it matter? This so-called expert is wrong." Josie said.

"Yes I think it does matter. Ivy is talking about socks and I've just googled it and she is right. I don't know about the rest of you but I'm here to learn about sock knitting from Ivy the expert. So I think we should let Ivy carry on without further interruptions." May said, staring at Josie. She was used to dealing with stroppy teenagers in her job as a teaching assistant and could certainly handle Josie.

There were a few hear-hears and well-saids effectively stopping Josie from saying more but everyone could see she was angry it looked as if she would burst with rage. If looks could kill thought May.

Talking Socks

Ivy carried on. "The first known socks were 'piloi' in Ancient Greece 8th century BC but they weren't knitted; they were made from matted animal hair. They were funny looking as they only had two toes so they could be worn with their sandals. I expect some of you have seen modern machine-knitted socks with all five toes knitted. The first knitted socks were made in Ancient Egypt and there is a pair in the Victoria & Albert museum. Check it out online when you have a minute. Socks can be knitted in various yarns depending on where you want to wear them . For wellingtons, thicker socks knitted with bulky yarn is better. For walking boots Merino wool. There are different fibres for knitting socks such as Alpaca, silk or cotton, even banana. For this workshop we are going to concentrate on knitting in 4ply yarns which are a mixture of wool and polyamide, they are soft but also hard wearing. As you can see they come in a wonderful array of colours, plain and patterns. We are going to use a basic sock knitting pattern. However, using some of these wonderful patterned yarns your socks will look anything but simple. Some of them knit up in a pattern or stripes without you having to do anything but plain knit. There are all sorts of combinations of colours you can choose, you can knit a contrast heel and toe or mix two colours. For your first pair of socks I suggest you keep to using one yarn so as not to get confused. I have knitted a sample swatch of some of the yarns so you can see how they knit up."

"I would have thought for the extortionate amount of money this course has cost us we should be taught more than basic sock knitting." Josie said with a sneer.

Ivy was about to speak and was thrown for a moment but wasn't going to get into another argument, she quickly recovered. "As I've already said in this workshop we will be knitting the basic sock pattern with these 4ply yarns. They will look anything but basic but in your own time you are free to knit whatever patterns you want. "

"Shove that where the sun doesn't shine," smirked Tony.

Ivy went on to talk about the different makes of yarns that were laid out in a dazzling paintbox of colours on her table. "Ok so that's the yarns," She paused and held up a pair of short circular needles. "I suggest that you all use these small circular needles, so you only have to knit continuously but some of you," she paused and held up four steel double ended needles, looked at Josie and repeated "But some of you may have brought your own or want to use four needles and that's fine. Now if you come up a table at a time you can choose your yarn and needles." Ivy turned to Evelyn and Alice on the closest table on her right, "ladies, would you like to come up first?"

Everyone was excited and May couldn't wait to get to the table and play with some delicious squishiness. She couldn't resist new yarn and had to stop herself going into yarn shops because she always found some new yarn to fall in love with. In her bedroom she had a cupboard full of works in progress and a yarn stash. At least now she didn't have a boyfriend she could spend more time knitting. Smiling at the thought of purchasing additional yarn to make more socks she was itching to get up to Ivy's table and hoped everyone would be quick at choosing their yarns and needles.

At Ivy's request, Evelyn and Alice started to rise from their chairs but before they could move to Ivy's table Josie got there first.

Evelyn hissed to Alice, "That bloody woman, I cannot believe she is here. I had enough of her on the last knitting holiday, she's so rude and she needn't think we've forgotten that she stole our pattern and published it as her own. I could murder her."

"Don't worry she'll get what's coming to her, Karma and all that." Alice replied."

"Not sure I can wait for Karma." Evelyn muttered sitting down again.

The others looked at them with sympathetic faces.

"Come along Mary," Josie gestured, waving her hand. Mary, clearly embarrassed by her sister but having no choice if she didn't want to make things worse, joined her at the table.

"As part of the workshop package, you may choose one skein of 100 grammes or two 50 gramme balls and a pair of needles."

"Seems to me we are not getting a lot for our money, what if I want to knit long socks?" Josie asked.

"You are welcome to purchase more yarn." Ivy said, folding her arms determined to stand her ground.

"Hurry up love we all want to get started" Tony called out then he turned to the others and whispered. "It's going to be a pain putting up with Madam Nastiness the whole week. I hope she's not going to spoil it for everybody. She'd better not pick on me and Michael or I'll be sorting her out."

"She reminds me of my mother," Lucy said sadly looking across at Josie.

"I must admit she is spoiling things for everyone. I've had a difficult time recently and I was hoping for a chilled out relaxing week. Tell you what if she carries on like that all afternoon we'll get her in the shell grotto and stab her with her knitting needles." May giggled and the others joined her.

"Is there a shell grotto here," asked Michael.

"Oh yes I believe so, the gardens are quite magnificent, there are fairy grottos and waterfalls. There isn't much time before dinner but before I go up to get ready I'm going to do a little exploring. I won't go far because we are having a proper tour of the gardens one morning with Mrs Jeffries."

"Can I join you tonight please?" Lucy asked.

"Of course," May smiled and looked across at Lucy and thought what a sweet woman she was.

Finally everyone had chosen their yarn and needles and cast on the required number of stitches and were attempting to rib in knit two purl two with varying degrees of success.

Sock Struggles

May looked across at Tony, poor thing was struggling. Ivy had to undo his sock three times and cast it on again for him. She even knitted the first two rows of rib to get him going. Michael was getting on fine if a little slow. They'd all giggled at his inability to knit without sticking his tongue out in concentration.

. . .

Ivy gave everyone individual attention throughout the afternoon. There was a break when tea and cake was brought out but the afternoon passed without further mishap to Ivy's relief. Ivy tapped on her tea mug to attract everyone's attention. "I hope you have enjoyed your first afternoon, I certainly have. You've all done really well, a great start. I'm really pleased, I hope you are," she looked nervously at Josie. "So that's the end of this afternoon's session. I expect you could do with stretching your legs after sitting here for three hours. You're welcome to stay here on the terrace or you may want to take a stroll around the splendid grounds which I recommend. Drinks will be served in the sitting room at six thirty prior to dinner at seven." I'll see you all tomorrow." Ivy started to load her yarns into a fabric storage box.

"Aren't you joining us for dinner Ivy?" Tony called out.

"No I'm afraid not."

"That's a shame come and join us tomorrow night, we'd all really love the chance to talk about all things woolly with you." May said.

"Ah that's really kind of you, perhaps I will tomorrow night."

"Come on then Lucy, let's take a little stroll around the garden." May gathered her knitting things and popped them in a project bag she had made especially for this week.

"Oh I love your little bag, it's adorable, where did you find it?" Lucy asked.

"I made it myself, I can share the pattern with you if you like?"

"Oh yes please, where did you get the fabric? It's so cute with the knitting cats." The two went of chattering and the others all left going in different directions.

Man's Ribbed Socks, warm and hard wearing

May agreed to meet Lucy in the hall before dinner as she was nervous of going in on her own. When they entered the sitting room they were greeted by Colonel Jeffries.

"Ah, at last some young girls to liven up the evening." He pressed a glass of sherry into both of their hands then picked up his glass and went behind putting an arm around each of them and forcing his way in between herding them to the side of the room

May removed his hot sweaty hand from her shoulder and took a step away. Poor Lucy looked really uncomfortable so May took her hand and pulled her away and next to her.

"Just being friendly. Oh dear. I see you two are the burn your bra lot, boring independent women." He air quoted the last two words, waving his glass around before taking a large swig of his whisky.

"I am sure Lucy will agree with me that we are both independent women but burning our bras was well before our time Colonel."

"Wouldn't do for me. Can't have the little woman thinking for herself, modern nonsense. Do you like my lovely home? Settling in? Anything you need, you just have to ask, we aim to please and I've never had any complaints yet." He grinned moving next to Lucy putting his arm around her waist and squeezing.

Lucy looked like the proverbial rabbit caught in the headlights.

May rescued her again, pulling her away. "Come on Lucy let's go and find Tony and Michael, see what sort of afternoon they've had.

"Aah already sussed out the men have you? Well done, that's what I like spirited girlies." The Colonel went to the bar and started to pour himself another large scotch.

"That's enough Gerald, you are making a spectacle of yourself. Do I need to remind you how important this week is ?" Ursula Jeffries hissed at him.

"All right old girl, keep your knickers on. Ah but you already do for me don't you?"

"That's enough! If you can't be civil then you will have to eat your dinner on your own and not with our guests in the dining room. I'm not letting you ruin this week so you had better buck up and you'd better leave those women alone too."

Luckily for the Colonel, Walters the butler announced dinner, saving him from his wife's wrath and the guests from further embarrassment.

"Ma'am dinner is served."

"Ma'am dinner is served," the colonel mimicked, "why does he never mention me?"

"I think you will find Gerald that you have to earn respect." Ursula Jeffries led the way into dinner and the others followed. The guests were looking at each other in astonishment as they had all overheard the exchange. The colonel was last through the door moving far too close behind Lucy.

"Let me show you to your seat my dear." He took her elbow and tried to seat her next to him but Ursula intercepted him with a nifty little move she had obviously used before.

"You are up here next to me dear, I hear you are a librarian and I want to know all about it, I'm an avid reader. Tony if you would like to sit here."

She pulled out the chair next to the Colonel for Tony and then shepherded Lucy to the other end next to her.

On the Terrace After Dinner

After an excellent dinner all the participants except for Josie and Mary moved to the outside terrace.

"Wow I'm stuffed, you certainly can't complain about the food, it was excellent don't you think?" Tony asked.

"And that pavlova was to die for," May said. "What about the Colonel and his wife's argy-bargy before dinner? That was embarrassing wasn't it?"

"He's embarrassing, fancy being married to him." Michael said.

"Yuck! I definitely don't want to think about it," May said, the others agreed.

Sheila and Hazel approached their table and Sheila asked, "Do you mind if we join you?"

They all murmured agreement and Tony jumped up, "Here let me fetch you some chairs." He borrowed two chairs from the next table along and they all shuffled around to make room. More drinks were fetched and soon they were all chatting away, sharing jokes and laughing. That was until a piercing shriek came from above.

"Will you stop that noise? There are decent people up here trying to sleep!" Josie's head retreated from the sash-window which she then slammed shut.

There was a moment's silence then everyone burst out laughing. Evelyn and Alice who had been sitting at a table on the far side of the terrace joined in the laughter and wandered over to join the others bringing their chairs with them.

"Room for two more?" Evelyn asked.

They all shuffled around again making room. Alice put their

bottle of wine on the table and held her glass up. "Cheers everyone, here's to a great week."

There was a chorus of cheers then May spoke. "I hate to speak ill of anyone but..."

"It is only half past nine, hardly bedtime and I think we are entitled to enjoy ourselves, after all we're paying for this holiday as much as she is." Tony said.

Evelyn put her glass down with a thump. " That woman is a nasty piece of work, we've been on a knitting holiday with her before."

"As well as being rude and unpleasant she stole an original pattern from us and is selling it as her own work." Alice said.

There were gasps from the others.

"Surely that's a breach of copyright," Lucy said.

"Exactly. We were on a knitting retreat in the Cotswolds and there was an extra hour workshop every day on designing one's own knitting pattern. Alice and I came up with a jumper pattern with a fancy yoke and knitted in the round so no seams to sew up."

"That sounds super, I hate sewing the seams up on my garments, they never seem to lie flat," Lucy said.

"Have you tried using a crochet hook to join your seams?" Alice asked.

"No, I wouldn't know how to." Lucy replied.

"We'd be happy to show you sometime this week and there are some good Youtube videos you can watch." Alice said.

"Oh what a shame I haven't got a television." Lucy said disappointed.

"Youtube is online, you don't need a tv." Tony said.

Lucy felt uncomfortable that she didn't have all these things that the others were taking for granted and vowed to herself that when she was home, she would get herself a tv and a smartphone.

"Tell us what happened about your knitting pattern Evelyn?" May asked.

"Well as I said we came up with this sweater design, it also had a special stitch pattern that Alice had discovered in a Japanese knitting dictionary. The tutor and others on the course thought it was really good. The tutor suggested we knitted a couple of test jumpers and if it worked out, she said we could sell the pattern. She even suggested we should design more, that we had a flair for it." Evelyn said proudly.

"On the last day in the afternoon there was a display of everybodies work achieved throughout the week. All the patterns that had been designed along with part- finished blankets which was what the retreat was about." Alice said

Evelyn jumped in. "A lovely afternoon tea was set on a long table in the middle of the garden for us to sit and eat together with smaller tables displaying our work around the outside."

They are like a tag team, thought May listening to them each telling a bit of the story.

"People finished eating at different times and then wandered around looking at each other's work." Alice said.

"And that's when she must have stolen our pattern." Evelyn said.

"What physically?" May asked.

"No, we think she must have taken photos on her phone." Alice said.

"Lots of people were taking photos of each other's work but only as ideas for colours and combinations of yarn." Evelyn said.

"Unfortunately we had displayed our pattern along with the blankets we had finished knitting so it was easy for her to take photos of the actual written pattern." Alice said.

"When we were back in Wales we both knitted a version of the sweater but didn't show each other until they were finished. They turned out brilliantly. Although the sweater design was simple and classic, with the addition of Alice's special stitch and the right yarn they looked fabulous." Evelyn paused for Alice to carry on.

"It was different and brought a unique aspect to the design, we knew we were onto a winner. We spent ages taking as professional photos as we could and we set up our own Etsy shop ." Evelyn said.

"We were amazed at the response and started selling the pattern really quickly." Alice said.

"Then came the bombshell. Someone contacted us saying that our pattern was already on sale on Etsy with another designer and we could be infringing copyright." Evelyn said.

"Don't tell us I expect we can all guess who was selling it." Tony said.

"What a nasty thing to do. Surely you could prove that it was your design first?" May asked.

"We could have challenged it but we thought it would be too difficult to prove." Alice said.

"We've chalked it up to experience and we won't let it happen again." Evelyn said, looking up at Josie's window." Alice said.

"Sometime this week we are going to challenge her over what she did. She cheated us." Evelyn said.

"Well we're not going to let her spoil this week for us are we," May said. "I can't stand bullies and I can't stand cheating. So we're with you ladies."

Tony, a little merry by now, jumped up with his glass in the air. "All for one and one for all, sock knitters united!"

The others all jumped up and joined him saying, "all for one and one for all, sock knitter united." They erupted into laughter again until May said, "Sorry to be a party pooper but I really need my bed now, so I'll say goodnight."

"Can I walk up with you?" Lucy asked.

"Of course." May looped her arm through Lucys and they walked off into the house.

The party broke up then and the rest of the guests made their way to their rooms.

The French Heel

Not long after the last of the guests had retired to bed the French doors opened and Mrs Jeffries came out followed by Walters. They made their way across the patio and into the garden, eventually stopping in the darkest spot surrounded by hedges and with a wooden bench. They sat and Walters put his arm around her, pulling her close, they kissed. She clung to him as he butterfly kissed down her neck. "I don't think I can carry on like this much longer, Ursula. I can't stand that idiot lording it over you, humiliating you in front of your guests. I swear I'll..."

"Hush my darling, be patient, it won't be forever the way he's drinking and smoking; he'll drop down dead at any moment with any luck."

He turned away from her and pounded his fist in his hand. "How can you bear it? Why haven't you kicked him out? He tricked you into marrying him. Wormed his way into your social circle, pretending to be an investment banker, splashed the cash, flash car, took you for posh meals and who was he really? A conman, that's who. I don't know how you could have been taken in by him." Walters put his hands on his knees and stared out into the garden.

"He caught me at a bad time, I'd not long lost my father and I had no idea what I was going to do. I was frightened. It's not as if I have any skills, I've never worked in my life. He was good looking, charming and made me feel cherished and don't forget I hadn't met you then. Of course I soon realised that it was all a front and when I started losing my friends after he lost them thousands in dodgy investments, that was the end for me. In nine short months he's emptied my bank account, mortgaged my home and all to feed his gambling habit. And now I'm forced to have strangers in my home in order to eat and pay the bills. It's insufferable." She put her face in her hands and sobbed.

Walters put his arm around her again and pulled her closer. "I'm sorry my darling, I didn't mean to upset you. Don't worry, I'll make sure he's out of your life soon."

"Pipe dreams. He won't leave here, why would he when he has my father's wine cellar to go through, a comfortable life and now we are taking in paying guests an income. Goodness knows what the guests make of him."

"Let's go to bed and forget about him for the night." He kissed her again, then arms entwined they made their way back to the house going in the same way they had come out through the kitchen garden, and the back door of the kitchen.

May's window had a view over the terrace and she was leaning on the window sill with her head out of the window when she saw Ursula and Walters emerge from the shrubbery. " Well, well, well, I don't suppose she was giving him instructions on where to plant the hollyhocks, naughty Mrs Jeffries." Smiling, she closed her curtains and went to bed.

Winding Wool

In the morning they all gathered for breakfast in the dining room. There were jugs of fruit juice and cold milk, cereals and pastries set out on one of the sideboards. A harassed looking woman in her forties wearing a crisp white chef's jacket, black and white chequered trousers and her dark hair pushed up under a cap entered the room.

"Good morning, my name is Nancy and I'm the chef. I don't know where that girl has got to this morning but she's not here where I need her. I can't find Walters to help me or Mrs Jeffries. So you are going to have to bear with me as I've got to cook your breakfast as well as serve it. Now I'll take your orders starting with you." She looked at Josie who was sitting on the end of the table nearest to her.

"I don't think it is very professional of you to come out here and tell us about your problems, after all we are paying guests." Josie sniffed and looked down her nose at Nancy.

"She's going to spit in her breakfast," whispered Tony.

Those close enough to him to hear tried not to laugh.

Nancy turned her back on Josie and asked Evelyn who was sitting opposite. "What would you like m'dear?"

"Egg, bacon, mushrooms and hash browns please."

"How would you like your egg, scrambled, fried or poached?"

"Whatever is easiest for you as you are on your own, I don't mind."

"Very good of you." Nancy went around everyone at the table until she arrived back at Josie who by now was spitting mad to be left to last.

"At last! I'll have two slices of crispy bacon, a sausage, roast tomatoes and a lightly poached but well cooked egg, and as you have made me wait till last I think I should have my breakfast first, don't you?"

Nancy didn't bother to reply but gave Josie a look that said everything about how she felt, turned and went to the door.

"Nancy, I am happy to help carry out the breakfasts for you if you like, it's no bother," May called out.

"I'll help too," Tony said.

You'll be right but that's very kind of you," Nancy said in her soft West country accent smiling at them, "If I get stuck I'll let you know. I'm hoping that wretched girl will turn up soon." She left the dining room.

"I would have expected a better class of staff, I shall have to complain to the Major." Josie said.

"Really why would you do an uncharitable thing like that. The poor woman is on her own, it's hardly her fault if the waitress doesn't turn up. It's not as if you are going to starve, give her a break." May said.

The others murmured their agreement which made Josie even crosser than she already was. "Get me some cereal Mary and don't drown it with milk."

May, who was sitting next to Mary, wanted to shout at the old bag to get her off her backside and get her own cereal but thought it would probably make things worse for Mary. No sooner had Josie finished eating her cereal she started drumming her fingers on the table and looking at the door, huffing every few minutes. The others ignored her and started chatting about this morning's excursion to Lynmouth. They were all looking forward to it, especially the ride on the famous cliff railway that connects Lynton and Lynmouth, the highest and steepest fully water powered Victorian railway in the world.

Jazz came in looking a little flustered, carrying two breakfasts. She placed them in front of Evelyn and Alice. "Morning everyone, sorry I was late but here is your breakfast." She hurried off and went to and fro from the kitchen with the plates of food. When she placed May's breakfast in front of her, May put a hand on her arm and stopped her.

"Is everything alright Jazz?"

"Yes, my nan was having a difficult morning and didn't want me to leave her."

"You look after your nan do you?"

"Yes, she used to be the cook here with the Jeffries family until the Colonel came along and sacked her. She hasn't been the same since. She's lost her way in life, she gets depressed."

"Stop chattering girl and fetch my breakfast, I'm not going to miss the excursion because of your laziness."

Poor Jazz looked like she was going to burst into tears, she'd had a bad morning with her nan, Nancy was cross with her and now she was getting it from a guest. They were all disgusted at Josie's comment but May couldn't contain herself. She was used to dealing with children and Josie was very childish and spoiled, but she waited until Jazz had left the room.

"How can you be so nasty, surely you can see the poor girl has had a difficult morning. You are not going to get your breakfast any quicker by being so rude."

"She'll probably spit in your breakfast," Tony chipped in, "and I wouldn't blame her."

The others not wanting to get involved put their heads down and tucked into their tasty breakfasts. Nancy brought Mary and Josie's breakfast in and she stood waiting whilst Jazz came in with a tray of toast in racks and shared them out on the table. She shepherded the young girl out in front of her, then looked at Josie, "kitchen's closed." and shut the door firmly behind her.

The others had stopped talking when Nancy came in, they realised she was looking out for the girl and had brought Josie's breakfast in herself to prevent her having another go. They all now watched Josie waiting for her to take her first bite. She was looking at her breakfast suspiciously for signs of tampering. In the end the seed Tony had planted won over and she threw down her napkin, pushed back her chair and said.

"Come along Mary, we need to get ready to go out." opening the door and waiting for Mary to join her.

May placed a hand on Mary's arm as she put down her knife and fork preparing to get up. "Why don't you eat your breakfast first Mary, the mini bus won't leave without us."

Mary hesitated, she knew she would get grief from Josie for not following her but the breakfast looked so good and these were nice people. She picked up her knife and fork and smiled at May. "I think I will this does look delicious."

The guests all enjoyed a splendid morning In Lynmouth with its incredible views, picturesque harbour, quaint cottages and lovely individual shops and cafes. The June weather was glorious and the group except for Josie and Mary met on the harbourside to enjoy the picnic that Nancy had provided. They all had individual brown paper bags with their choice of fruit, sandwiches and a muffin. Tony and Michael were heroes and went and fetched take-away teas and coffees for everyone and they all agreed it was a splendid trip.

When they arrived back at Merton Manor they had an hour to rest before the afternoon workshop started. May took her kindle and left her room wanting to spend a quiet hour reading in the garden. She was walking through the hallway when she saw a door ajar, it had never been open before and feeling curious she gently pushed it open and looked inside. It was a library come study with rows of leather bound books behind glass. Fascinated as a lover of books she moved further into the room only to discover the Colonel and Nancy the chef in what can only be described as a compromising situation. They didn't hear her and she quietly back-tracked out of the room, only to come face to face with Ursula who pushed past her and went in. May waited for the fireworks but Ursula had firmly shut the door behind her so she could only hear muffled raised voices through the thick oak door.

Knitting on the Terrace

The afternoon knitting session was in full swing, the sunny June weather meant they were all on the terrace again. On the tables were glasses, large jugs of water with ice and lemon and small tubs of talcum powder for hands if they become hot and sticky.

tIvy arrived and placed her plastic tub on the ground next to her table. "Afternoon everyone, I hear you had a lovely morning in Lynmouth. It's a very special place, one of my favourites. This afternoon I am going to come around to you individually to make sure your socks are coming along correctly. Some of you will have finished the rib and moved onto the plain knitting. Others might still be working on the rib and that's fine. I'm also going to lay out some finished socks on my table, feel free to come up and take a look. It should inspire you to want to knit more socks and eventually knit a variety of patterns and colour changes such as a different colour rib and toe. You will also see different lengths of socks, there are some shorties with a rib and shorties with a roll-top. I shall be talking more about these later in the week."

"I need your help over here," Josie called out.

"She's such a pain, why does she always have to be first with everything?" Tony asked.

"Perhaps she had a deprived childhood," Michael answered.

"Mary must have had the same childhood and she's not like Josie," Lucy pointed out.

"That's true but she is obviously a very unhappy woman, something must have made her like it." May said.

"That may be so but there is no need to make others unhappy by being nasty. I thought that after what we've all been through the last three years with Covid we were all trying to be kind to each other." Tony said.

"I don't think Josie received the memo," May said chuckling, "Let's all keep smiling at her and being really nice, we might convert her."

The others laughed and agreed to give it a go.

Ivy joined them, pulling up a chair. "Well you all seem to be enjoying yourselves, how are the socks coming on?"

May and Lucy had finished their ribbing and had moved on to the plain knitting. Ivy turned to Tony. "So how are you doing with your ribbing Tony?"

"It's crap. I know it doesn't look like it should." Tony threw his sock down in disgust.

Ivy picked up the offending knitting. "It's not that bad, I think you are miscounting the knit two purl two. So, you have three choices, one, you could undo it all and start again, two, you could carry on but getting it right from now on or three, you could undo it and knit a roll down top."

"What do you think I should do?" Tony asked.

"As it's your first sock I would carry on, I'm sure you will be happy to wear it even if the first stitches are a bit awry. Let me get you straight and I'll show you again how you can check if your next stitch should be knit or purl."

"Go on then, I don't mind if it's a bit wrong."

"Okay, so I'm going to knit a few rows for you to get you back on track."

They all watched as Ivy's fingers and needles flew. "Right now if you look you can see what's happening. The rib has an elasticated effect which holds the sock up and that's formed by the knit two, purl two rib. The purl is a horizontal line like a step and the knit is like an arch window in a church. Now you have a go." Ivy handed the sock over.

"I'm very slow compared to May and Lucy but mine is correct I think," Michael showed his sock to Ivy.

"It's not a race Michael , it's all about enjoying the process and your knitting is perfect well done."

"Ooh goody two-shoes," Tony said with a grin.

The others all laughed. Ivy went back to her table and Jazz and Walters brought out trays of tea paraphernalia and plates of homemade lemon drizzle cake and shortbread biscuits.

Ivy banged the table with the ends of her scissors to get everyone's attention. " Whilst we drink our tea and eat some of the delicious cake and biscuits I just want to say well done everyone, I'm really impressed with your socks so far."

She was interrupted by Josie who accosted Jazz as she was bringing in more tea and cake. "You girl, I don't like this cake, it's too lemony. Fetch me something else."

Jazz ignored her and carried on with delivering her trays before turning back towards the kitchen, stopping next to Josie. "My name is Jazz, not girl. There are three choices here and I don't think there are any more alternatives." Jazz walked off two spots of bright red colour on her cheeks.

"Wow, Josie needs to watch it, Jazz is one angry woman."

Jazz came back with a slice of seed cake on a plate, puts it down heavily in front of Josie and hurried off

"I can't eat this, it's got seeds in it, they'll get stuck in my teeth."

"Pity they don't get stuck in her throat." Tony murmured.

"It's only fit for the birds." Josie picked the cake up and threw it into the garden. When she thought everyone was looking at Ivy, she took a large slice of lemon drizzle cake, and four shortbread biscuits.

. . .

Ivy waited until everyone had finished eating. "I know that some of you have looked at my example socks. Now I'm going to talk you through a couple of them. This pair is knitted using the basic four ply sock pattern with a rib cuff and a self-striping yarn. It's like magic especially if you are a beginner knitter and want a more exciting sock." Ivy held up a colourful stripy sock, showing it around. Then she picked up another pair. "These are shorty socks and have a very short rib. They are ideal for trainers. You can also knit this without a rib and as you can see from this pair, only using knit stitch you get a nice roll top effect. A roll top sock is ideal for people who have problems with their circulation or water retention as they aren't tight and don't constrict the leg. I've knitted this next pair with a contrasting cuff and toe, really simple but very effective. So using the basic sock pattern you can make a variety of very different socks. Once you are comfortable and enjoy knitting socks you won't want to stop. I know I am always eager to start a new pair with new yarn. It's so exciting to see how they knit up. I will let you get back to your socks now but I'm going to move around the group helping where it's needed."

"Tony started clapping and they all joined in except Josie who remarked. "Ridiculous clapping like seals. Anyone would think she's done a song and a dance act."

The rest of the afternoon passed with pleasant chatter and knitting until it was time to pack away and go to their rooms and get ready for dinner.

I could get used to this May thought, as she lay in the roll-top bath looking out over the garden. She had used plenty of the luxury smellies provided and was feeling very relaxed, it was only as she was getting out half an hour later that she realised she hadn't thought of Eddie at all today, progress.

Comparative Tensions

Everyone gathered in the sitting room for drinks prior to dinner. To May's surprise the man she had met on her first day was there. The Colonel was in full raconteur mode entertaining everyone with amusing stories of his travels. May and Lucy were on the periphery of the group not wanting to get too close to the Colonel. Sheila and Hazel, two women very comfortable with who they were, had no such qualms about being close enough to the Colonel's wandering hands finding him hilarious and his attempts at flirtation even funnier, slapping his hands away with glee. As the group moved away from the bar May and Lucy moved in leaning their elbows on the counter.

"Good evening ladies,I don't think we've been introduced. I'm Ryder the Colonel's nephew." He had watched them enter the room and was ready with two full cocktail glasses, one of which was meant for himself but moving next to May he offered one to her and one to Lucy, looking at them expectantly.

May glanced at Lucy who was seemingly transfixed. "I'm May and this is," she turned to Lucy who panicked, took a huge gulp of her cocktail, swallowed then coughed and spluttered as the strong alcohol hit the back of her throat. "This is Lucy and I think your cocktail may be a little strong for her taste." May patted Lucy on the back.

"What about you, is it too strong for you?" Rhyder asked, holding her gaze.

May smiled, he really did have the most amazing eyes. Her gaze moved down to his lips and further, enjoying the sight of his toned chest and strong arms revealed by the tight white polo shirt he wore, obviously designer. Stopping herself from looking down further she took a sip of her drink. "Mmn perfect. Passionfruit?"

"Good guess, passionfruit martini." Ryder raised an eyebrow and moved closer, leaning his back against the bar, his arm and hip touching hers.

May's stomach did a flip, heat rose between them and whatever cologne he was wearing, something citrusy, heightened her senses. She did like a man who smelled good and Ryder smelled very good. A little flirtation was just what she needed. She wasn't naive, she knew exactly what sort of man Ryder is but she would be leaving here in a few days and she intended to enjoy herself. Looking up into his incredible blue eyes, were those contacts? She lowered her glass leaving a drop on her lower lip, which she ran her tongue over. His eyes darkened as he focused on her mouth.

"Here's my two luscious girlies. You two are making this week worthwhile. Too many wrinkled oldies on this knitting malarkey for me." The Colonel's hot hands snaked around May's and Lucy's waist, his whisky breath assaulted their cheeks as he squeezed between them. He pulled them away from the bar. "You'd better watch out for this randy charmer girlies, he takes after his uncle, a regular hit with the ladies." He cupped both their bottoms with his sweaty hands. "He'll be in your knickers before you can say…"

. . .

May scraped her heel down the Colonel's shin, the pain made him bend over as he did she stuck her elbow out connecting with his nose with a crunch. As blood spurted from his nose, he shouted obscenities at May. Shocked at what she'd done, she grabbed hold of Lucy's arm and hung on as Ursula came running over.

"I'm really sorry. I didn't mean to hurt him but it was instinctive. In my defence he was touching us inappropriately." May said.

Ryder had grabbed a bar towel, folded it and pressed it against the Colonel's nose. "Shut up Unkie you're making things worse."

Ursula had witnessed his pervy behaviour before but she had never seen him go as far as touching the women. She was furious but not with May. She was angry and embarrassed at her clown of a husband, how could she have been fooled as to what sort of man he really is. What on earth would the guests think? Those women would be quite entitled to make a formal complaint, this could be the end of my business before it's really got started.

Ryder, with a wink at May, grabbed his uncle by the arm and led him away to get cleaned up. They could still hear him complaining as Ryder pulled him along.

Rescuing the Situation

"Ladies, I am so sorry. Please accept my apologies for my husband's unacceptable behaviour, he gets very silly after a few drinks. I'm hoping you will forgive his momentary lapse in judgement. I promise you it won't happen again." Ursula said, shaking with nerves.

May was relieved Ursula had condemned the Colonel's behaviour, she was worried she had gone too far but instinct had taken over. The whole room had gone silent after the incident.

"Are you okay with that Lucy?" May looked at her.

Lucy, clearly still upset, nodded. May looked around and found Michael, giving him a pleading look. With her arm still slipped through Lucy's, she gave her a side hug whilst talking. "Michael and I are very interested in your garden Ursula, especially the history, aren't we Michael?"

Michael thankfully immediately came to her rescue. "Yes, absolutely, I'm a very keen gardener myself. Your gardens are absolutely stunning Ursula and I'm very much looking forward to the tour and learning more about the history of how they came about."

May, mouthed a silent thank you to Michael. Ursula's face lost some of its tension and she was clearly relieved at the change of subject. Her eyes lost their dull look as she enthused about the gardens her grandfather had had designed by Humphrey Repton. "Tomorrow morning's activity is a tour of the gardens and you will also be able to see Repton's red book which contains his watercolour painting of the gardens before and after the proposed design."

"That sounds lovely," May said, "I love gardens and yours is exceptional."

"I'm very lucky with my gardeners, they keep them looking beautiful, we do have plants for sale so that guests can take a little bit of Merton Manor home."

"That's a lovely idea. I would like to take a plant home for my garden." Lucy said.

"I would if I had a garden of my own but I live with my parents and the garden is sacrosanct. They are both fantical gardeners and I swear they know every single plant there. I wouldn't dare try and plant one of my own. I'm not allowed to do anything but sit in it but that's okay. " May said.

"Perhaps you could gift them one of our Heritage plants, they are unlikely to have one of those." Ursula said.

"Now that's a really good idea. We must visit the plant shop together before we leave Lucy." May said.

. . .

Dinner is Served

Walters stood in the doorway and rang the gong signalling dinner was ready and they all moved through into the dining room. This evening Sheila and Hazel ended up on either side of the Colonel who was already seated in his chair looking slightly worse for wear. Over the bridge of his nose he had a sticking plaster which did little to conceal his red and swollen nose. Apart from sounding a little nasal he was drinking whisky and seemed to be back to his old self, exuding good humour and bonhomie.

May followed close to Ursula intending to sit next to her and carry on the conversation as she really wanted to know more about the history of the house. As they reached the table Josie pushed in front of her and plomped herself down on the chair next to Ursula, giving May a triumphant smile.

"Rude or what," May said under her breath, turning and looking for a seat away from the wretched woman.

After dinner the group except for Josie, Mary and Ursula gathered on the terrace. The Colonel had dispensed drinks at the bar and joined them continuing his role as entertainer for the night. May and Lucy sat in seats out of reach and after about ten minutes Mary stepped onto the terrace looking nervous. May spotted her and called her over. "Hi Mary, come and join us, would you like a drink?"

"The Colonel jumped up and offered Mary his seat. "There you are m'dear, you sit there and I'll get you a drink." He left for the bar.

"He might be a bit of a lech but at least he has manners. I'm glad you joined us tonight Mary, It's a long time to spend in your room if you go straight up there after dinner. Much better to be out here enjoying the evening whilst this lovely weather holds." May said.

"Especially in this beautiful garden with pleasant company." Mary agreed.

The Colonel came back and handed Mary a tall glass of gin and tonic with ice and a slice. "There you are my dear, chin, chin.

Move over ladies." He pulled up another chair and tried to squeeze in between May and Lucy. May rolled her eyes at Tony.

"Over here Colonel, we've made a space," Tony said, budging his chair up.

The Colonel, clearly disappointed but realising he'd been outwitted, made his way to the chair Tony had placed for him and sat down. A relieved Lucy smiled gratefully at Tony. The conversation flowed as did the drinks until the clock in the sitting room chimed eleven o'clock.

Mary rose. "That's me done, I'm ready for my bed. Thank you for the pleasant company, good night."

"What a lovely woman," May said. That's the first time we've had a chance to really talk to her. I'm off too, do you want to walk up with me Lucy?"

"Yes please, night everyone." Lucy said following May through the open french windows, where Walters was waiting to come out a tray in his hands.

There was a chorus of goodnights and the party broke up, everyone leaving except the Colonel and Walters.

"Your nightcap Colonel." Walters poured a small measure in a fresh glass, placing it on the table and standing the Whisky decanter next to it. He picked up the Colonel's used glass and a few empty glasses that were left scattered about the tables and saying goodnight to the Colonel left the terrace.

There wasn't a sound from the house, everybody was tucked away safely in their beds. The only sounds in the garden were the occasional hoot of an owl and screech of a fox. The Colonel lit a cigar watching the smoke curling up into the night. This is the life he thought. This is where I was always meant to be, he didn't allow himself to think back to his humble beginnings. Leaning back in his chair he downed his whisky musing on an enjoyable evening. I don't know why Ursula makes such a fuss about having paying guests, especially when some of them are young and juicy. Mind you that plump one's got a bit of fire in her, I like that in my women. She went a bit far this evening but I bet I can tame her. Having company is a vast improvement on our usual boring evenings with Ursula scowling at me every time I get another drink. I virtually have to live in my study because it's the only place I can watch the gg's on the tv and drink without being told off . Picking up the decanter he poured himself another whisky, a large measure.

Shaping By Casting Off

May woke early, she lay there for a few moments then checked her phone; surprised to find how early it was, only half past six. Knowing she wouldn't be able to go back to sleep she decided to have a soak in the bath, and read her book. She poured in some of the luxurious smellies provided and ran the taps. It was another glorious morning so as she climbed into the bath before she sat down she opened the sash-window and stuck her head out. She caught sight of someone sitting on the edge of the terrace. Leaning further out she realised it was the Colonel and he was sitting in the same chair he had been in last night. That's a bit odd she thought, he must have drunk himself to sleep. She quietly pulled down the window a little and sunk down into the delicious hot soapy water, soon forgetting the Colonel as she lost herself in her cosy murder mystery book.

She had been in the bath for about half an hour, topping it up with hot water as the water cooled. Looking at her prune-like fingers she had decided she'd had enough and was about to get out when a piercing scream wrenched through the quiet morning.

May dropped her book in the water and shot to her feet, water sloshed over the edge of the bath. The scream had come from the garden. She slid the window further up and poked her head out. Nancy was draped over the Colonel and was sobbing loudly. Other heads popped out of their windows but May pulled back, climbed out of the bath, grabbed her robe and left her room, running down the stairs in her bare feet and through the hall to the sitting room. Unfortunately the french doors were locked and she struggled with the key in her haste but eventually she was outside. "Nancy, what on earth has happened?"

"He's dead, my darling man is dead. But he can't be dead, we love each other, we were going to get married." She howled.

"Hush, hush," May put her arms around Nancy and pulled her off, luckily Lucy arrived. "Take her for me Lucy, sit her down and try to keep her calm. If she starts talking about her and the Colonel being in love, try and distract her. That's the last thing his wife needs to hear when she arrives."

Lucy took the sobbing woman across to the other side of the terrace and sat her down, thrusting some napkins she'd grabbed off the table into Nancy's hands. The other guests roused by all the noise poured through the French doors but stopped at the sight of the Colonel. Ursula and Walters, both in dressing gowns, pushed through the others to see what was going on. When they saw the Colonel they both looked at each other.

Coming to her senses Ursula said, "Oh my God! Is he dead?" She gasped, grabbing Walters who put his arm around her waist and held her firmly. She put her hands up and threaded her fingers through her hair which was loose and obviously hadn't seen a brush that morning. "I tried to get him to stop drinking and smoking. I knew it would kill him in the end."

Walters sat Ursula down on one of the patio chairs and moved closer to the Colonel. "Are you sure he's dead?"

May had checked for a pulse but clearly the Colonel had been dead for some time. " Yes I'm sure. We need to call his doctor. Can you find the number for us Walters?"

"Yes, I'll call him," Walters walked back into the house.

May walked over to Ursula. "I'm so sorry Ursula."

Nancy pulled away from Lucy and confronted Ursula. "Don't you dare say sorry to her, she's not sorry. She's glad to see him dead. She made his life a misery. He loved me, we were going to be married." She started sobbing again.

"You ridiculous woman. Why on earth do you think he would marry you? I think you forget he was my husband. You are stupid if you believed his lies. That's what he told all his women, you were one in a long line. I'm not listening to this drivel, I'm going up to get dressed." Ursula got up and turned her back on Nancy walking towards the French windows. Nancy ran towards her and grabbed her arm pulling her back and shaking her. "You bitch. You're lying. There were no other women. He only loved me." Every sentence screeched with a shake of Ursula.

May ran to Nancy and tried to release her hold on Ursula,Tony, Sheila and Hazel came to help.

"This is not going to help Nancy. Let her go. The Colonel wouldn't want this." May said, trying to prise Nancy's fingers away.

"May's right let go Nancy. Come and tell me all about it. Come on there's a dear." Tony's powers of persuasion were obviously better than Mays as Nancy finally let go and turned to Tony sobbing into his chest.

"I'll take her to the kitchen and make some tea." Tony said

"We'll all come and help ." Michael said.

Sheila, Hazel, Evelyn and Alice, not keen to stay on the terrace with a dead body, followed Michael. Mary went to follow the others but Josie stopped her.

"We are paying guests and we certainly are not going to sit in the kitchen. Come along Mary, we'll go to our rooms and dress. There had better be some breakfast ready for us in the dining room when we come back down."

"We can help with the breakfasts too." Michael added.

May and Ursula were the only ones left on the patio.

"Are you okay?" May asked rubbing Ursula's arm where Nancy had gripped it so viciously.

Ursula shook her off her. "I'm fine, I'm going up to get dressed and then I'm coming down to give that woman the sack."

"Ursula, hang on a minute. I know I'm a guest and probably shouldn't be speaking out of turn but this is your home, your business and you've just lost your husband. I can't even imagine how you are feeling right now but I don't think you should make any hasty decisions. This may seem a bit heartless but you have paying guests, so as I see it you have two choices. You can send us home and refund all our money." May saw Ursula's eyes widen at the thought of having to pay back all the money. "Or we can stay and you keep the money. To do that the guests need to be fed and that means you need a cook unless you want to do the cooking. Before you say anything here me out. The GP will be here soon and the police, they will expect everyone to still be here."

"The Police! Why on earth would the police come, there's nothing suspicious. Clearly he had a heart attack?" Ursula sat down hard on the nearest chair.

Walters looked out from behind a bush next to the terrace and saw Ursula near the French windows engrossed in talking to one of the guests. Moving swiftly he stepped out from the bush and onto the edge of the terrace. Averting his eyes from the Colonel's body he picked up the decanter off the table and was bracing himself to turn and pick up the glass when he saw Ursula stand up. Swiftly he moved back behind the bush where he could see them but they couldn't see him.

May looked at Ursula's shocked face but she had read enough murder mysteries to know the procedure even when a natural death occurred in someones home. It was just as well she had mentioned the police and prepared Ursula for what was to come. "The Colonel's death was sudden and unexpected and the police always attend a sudden death. It is going to be a busy and difficult time for you and as I say I know I'm speaking out of turn but I suspect that the reason you have turned your home into a hotel is because you need the money. I really want to stay because I'm having a great time and really enjoying the knitting workshop, the good food and your lovely home."

Ursula sat up straighter, two spots of colour in her cheeks. "How dare you."

May knew it wasn't her place to tell Ursula what to do but as there was no one else she felt she had no choice. "As I say it's up to you but it seems to me that keeping this week's retreat going, keeping your guests fed and happy and keeping the large amount of money they've paid which has probably been spent or earmarked for bills, makes sense." May stopped knowing she'd said enough. She turned and looked at the Colonel one more time after a few seconds she realised something was different. Then she realised what it was, funny she thought, I'm sure there was a decanter on the table, where did it go? Shrugging thinking she must have been mistaken, she left Ursula and went upstairs to her room to get dressed.

Ursula dry-eyed got up and walked across the terrace stopping a couple of feet away from the body of her husband, covering her nose and mouth with her hand. It looked like he had fallen asleep. One arm hung over the arm of the chair, his cigar had burnt down to nothing leaving burn marks between his fingers. The other hand lay draped on his thigh, a whisky tumbler rested on his groin. Forcing herself to move she drew closer. She looked at his nicotine stained moustache, his fleshy lips and sagging jowls and felt no love, loss or grief, all she felt was relief.

Walters watched Ursula draw closer to the Colonel he was about to call out and let her know he was there when to his astonishment

she looked around then, carefully she picked the whisky glass up, slipped it in her dressing gown pocket and swiftly made her way back through the French doors.

Thank goodness nobody had seen either of us he thought as

he made his way across the Terrace towards the back door of the kitchen.

But someone had been watching and had seen Walters remove the decanter and Ursula remove the glass.

Provisional Cast On

May followed the noisy chatter coming from the kitchen and found quite a jolly scene considering there was a dead body not far away. Ryder, Tony, and the other woman were sitting around a large rectangular table tucking into what looked to May's hungry eyes a full English breakfast.

"Do you want a cooked breakfast?" Michael asked, holding a plate of food that sent May's mouth watering. "Here you have mine and I'll have the next one." He pushed the plate into May's hands. "Go and sit down, everythings taken care of."

"Come and sit over here May," Ryder said, nodding his head towards the spare chair next to him and looking at her with a smirk as if to dare her to sit there.

Knowing she was giving in but not caring she went and sat down next to him. "Morning, I'm very sorry about your Uncle."

Ryder shuffled his chair closer, his warm thigh pushing against hers. "Yes it's very sad, poor old bugger. Unkie was a nightmare but I didn't want to see him dead although I'm sure that others did." Ryder said loudly at the same time as Walters came into the kitchen.

"What's that supposed to mean?" Walters asked.

"It means what I said." Ryder answered, staring at Walters

until the other man looked away then resumed eating his breakfast.

"Awkward," Tony said.

The tension was broken by Mary knocking timidly on the kitchen door. "I'm really sorry to trouble you and I hate to ask but Josie is sitting in the dining room waiting for her breakfast."

"Tell her to get off her snippy little arse and get in here if she wants breakfast." Nancy shouted, banging the heavy frying pan down on the top of the aga.

Poor Mary hovered in the doorway looking as if she was going to burst into tears. Ursula came up behind her and cleared her throat to let her know she was there. "Mary, I apologise for the wait, please go back and tell Josie breakfast is on its way."

Mary, clearly grateful that she didn't have to go back and tell Josie that she had to have her breakfast in the kitchen, smiled at Ursula. "Thank you."

"Ah here comes the Merry Widow. Surely you aren't going to soil those tender hands of yours by serving breakfast Ursula?" Ryder said, smiling as he leaned back on his chair and balancing on the rear two legs.

Ursula ignored Ryder and busied herself making up a tray with teapot, milk jug, sugar pot and cups and saucers. Then she poured boiling water on the tea bags and popped the lids on. She fetched some orange juice from the fridge and poured two glasses, setting them down on the tray with the tea things. Before she could pick the tray up Walters was by her side, he picked it up and left for the dining room.

"There you go Ursula, rescued from drudgery by your knight in shining armour." Ryder dropped his chair back on its four legs with a bang.

You could have cut the atmosphere with a knife when Walters returned to the kitchen. He gave Nancy the order for Josie and Mary's cooked breakfasts then proceeded to put bread in the toaster and make curls of butter in a dish.

The guests had gone quiet not sure what was going on but

realising there were all sorts of tensions between Ryder, Walters, Ursula and Nancy. They carried on eating, shooting glances at each other and waiting for the next piece of drama.

Ursula poured herself a cup of tea and walked to the head of the table. "Thank you all for helping out this morning, we, I, really appreciate it. This tragedy has blighted what should have been a calm, restful retreat and I am really sorry. I quite understand if some of you decide to leave. If you do, you will receive a partial refund for the days you have lost. For those of you who decide to stay, I will do my utmost to ensure the rest of the week goes smoothly and enjoyably for you all. Hopefully we can go ahead with this morning's tour of the gardens at ten thirty or as soon as possible. I am going to my room now but one of my staff will call me down to reception for those of you who wish to leave."

Her colour high but still maintaining her dignity, Ursula picked up her cup and saucer and walked to the door but before she got there, May called after her. "Ursula, we are all really sorry for your loss. We admire your courage and appreciate your willingness to carry on. I for one would like to stay, up until now I've been having a fantastic time and I'm looking forward to learning more about the gardens."

There was a chorus of agreement from the other guests at the table and Ursula was clearly moved. "Thank you, that means a lot." She slipped out of the door quietly. Ryder followed her.

As soon as the door had closed there was a low hum as they all started discreetly chattering to each other about the Colonel's death. They were interrupted when the back door into the kitchen was suddenly flung open on its hinges, hitting the doorstop with a bang. Jazz followed it chattering nineteen to the dozen. " Morning Nancy, cor what a morning . Nan took forever to eat her breakfast, the cat threw up on the rug and then when I was about to leave I found my bike had a puncture. I was lucky that my uncle, he's the postman, turned up and took pity on me and gave me a lift." She suddenly realised there were more people than Nancy in the kitchen. "Whoa what's going on here? Why are you all eating in the kitchen?"

Michael, who was walking away from the oven with his breakfast and was closest to Jazz, quietly told her the news. Nancy moved over to the large butler sink with the heavy frying pan dropping it into the hot foamy suds keeping her back to them. Nancy was fussy about her special pans and insisted on washing them herself. Jazz's job was to stack the dishwasher and clean any other cooking pots.

"Well I'm not going to shed any tears over the old bastard." Jazz said, taking her apron off the back door and tying it on. She poured herself a mug of tea and walked close to the breakfast table. "Good riddance I say!"

May flapped her hand at Jazz. "Keep your voice down , Nancy is very upset."

Tony, unable to resist sharing the gossip, waved her over. "Apparently she's been having an affair with the Colonel and she thought they were going to get married." His eyebrows shot up his forehead as he nodded to emphasise the scandal.

Jazz snorted and bending closer to the table in a low voice said. "I don't think so. Last week Nancy gave him an ultimatum and they had a humongous row. She said he had to tell Ursula he wanted a divorce and that he was going to marry her or else she would tell Ursula herself. He laughed in her face and told her to go ahead. He said Ursula knew all about his dalliances as he put it and that Nancy wasn't the only one and she was a fool for thinking he'd marry someone like her." Jazz was clearly enjoying sharing this juicy gossip. She moved her head closer to the others and whispered. He got really nasty, he said, 'why, when I can have any number of beautiful slim elegant women that I want, would I choose you? When you're naked you look like one of your round suet dumplings'. I mean that's really cruel isn't it? I was in the larder at the time, I think she had forgotten I was in there when the Colonel came in. I was peering through the gap between the larder door and the frame and I saw her pick up the cast iron frying pan with both hands and hold it up in the air. I was really scared because she was in such a rage. I thought she was going to kill him so I jumped out and shouted at her that he wasn't worth it." Jazz explained in one long gush of words.

"God, that's awful, how could he have been so cruel? Still, I think she must still love him because she was very upset this morning." May said.

"I'd better go and help her." Jazz said.

May was disappointed she knew it was bad but she'd been hoping for some more gossip but before Jazz could go to help Nancy the reception bell went so she had to leave to go and to see who it was.

The Round Toe

When Jazz arrived at reception it was to find a short tubby man in a grey suit and with a leather doctors bag.

"Good morning, I'm Doctor Hughes, is Mrs Jeffries about?"

"Yes Doctor, I'll just call her." Jazz's hand was shaking as she picked up the phone and pressed a button. "The doctor is here Mrs Jeffries. Yes of course." Jazz put the phone down and addressed the doctor. She says she will be down in a few minutes, Doctor."

"Oh that's okay, I'll meet her up there, which one is the Colonel's room?"

Jazz realised that the doctor thought the Colonel's body was in his bedroom. It was an easy assumption to make but she didn't want to be the one to have to explain where he was and where he'd been all night to her relief Mrs Jeffries appeared.

"Good morning Doctor."

"My sincere condolences Mrs Jeffries. I must admit to being very surprised to hear that the Colonel had passed, he was as fit as a fiddle when I saw him last week."

Mrs Jeffries' complexion paled at the doctor's words. "I didn't know he had been to see you recently, doctor."

"Oh, only routine, you know, had to check him over before his repeat prescription could carry on." He laughed and winked at her. "The magic little blue pills. Life in the old dog yet hey?" Doctor Hughes realised he had probably spoken out of turn. "My apologies."

Mrs Jeffries went from pale to flushed, aware that Jazz was listening to every word. She turned to her and said, "Jazz, go back to the kitchen and help with the breakfasts."

Jazz rushed off a huge grin on her face, eager to share this juicy tidbit of gossip.

"Shall we go up to your bedroom?" The Doctor asked.

Colour fled from Mrs Jeffries face again as she thought of the fact that the Colonel's body was not lying in his bed wearing his M & S pyjamas but was in fact still wearing his clothes from yesterday and had been sitting out on the terrace all night. She realised it was going to look rather odd to the doctor. Pulling her shoulders back and drawing herself up she said. "I am afraid he is not in his bedroom but outside on the terrace. I fear he may have been there all night. Follow me." She led the way down the hall, through the sitting room and out of the French windows onto the terrace. She pointed across to the Colonel. " I'll wait for you in my office if that's alright Doctor? As you can imagine this morning has been extremely upsetting."

"Yes, yes, of course m'dear." Doctor Hughes wondered what on earth had happened, had there been an accident?. He walked slowly across the terrace. The smell hit him within a few feet. There was no doubt the Colonel was dead. He stood in front of the Colonel's body. "What happened to you then old chap?"

He didn't really need to check the Colonel's pulse to see if he was dead because just by looking at him he could tell but duty dictated he did. The Colonel's complexion had taken on a deathly pale colour and rigour mortis had set in. A squeak and a fart made Dr Hughes start, the result of the digestive gases escaping the body. The Colonel was fully dressed and slouched back in the chair. The doctor superficially checked the body over without disturbing anything. From external appearances it looked to him as if the Colonel had had a heart attack but there were a few things that worried him. He made a quick call on his mobile phone before going back to the sitting room and closing the French doors. He used a tissue wrapped around the key to lock the doors which he then put in his bag ready to hand over to the police. He would be very happy to pass over the responsibility and let them make all the decisions regarding the Colonel.

He found Mrs Jeffries in her office behind the reception desk. She stood up as he walked in.

"Come in doctor, take my seat, you can use the desk to write on. Can I get you a cup of tea or coffee?"

"I'm afraid I won't be able to write the death certificate, Mrs Jeffries."

Her hand flew to her chest. "I don't understand? I've been telling him for months he'd have a heart attack from smoking and drinking too much."

" I'm afraid the Colonel's had what we call an unexpected or unexplained death." He put his hand up to stop Mrs Jeffrie from interrupting. "I'm not saying there is anything suspicious about his death but I only saw him last week and he was perfectly healthy. I wouldn't have expected him to die so suddenly. In this situation I am obliged to call in the police and the coroner will need to be informed. I must warn you that there may have to be an autopsy."

Mrs Jeffries dropped into her chair, her face as white as a sheet. The door opened and Walters came in.

"Ursula, what's happened? Are you alright?" He rushed to her side, crouched beside her chair, put his arm around her and kissed the top of her head. "It's alright sweetheart."

Flustered at his sign of affection in front of the doctor she roughly pushed him away. "I'm alright Walters but the doctor has informed me that the police have to be called in as the Colonels is an unexpected death. It's all very upsetting."

Walters moved away but kept his concerned gaze on Ursula.

Well, well, well, looks like there's something more going on here thought Doctor Hughes. He was surprised at the familiarity between Walters and Ursula as she had only been married to the Colonel a short while.

"That's ridiculous, surely he drank himself to death. It must have been a heart attack?" Walters protested.

Doctor Hughes wasn't amused at having his judgement questioned especially by a glorified butler and he wasn't going to stand for it. He stood up. "Mrs Jeffries, until the police arrive I must ask that nobody enters the garden terrace until they say so. I will wait outside for them. You should wait here as they will want to speak with you when they arrive." With a hard stare at Walters he left the room.

"You idiot, what do you think he's going to surmise with you rushing in and kissing me. The last thing we want now is everyone knowing about us. We need to stay calm and you need to keep your place as an employee. " Ursula said, pacing the floor of the office.

Walters grabbed her arm in a vice-like grip, his fingers digging into the soft flesh of her arm stopping her pacing. "Keep my place." The words dripped from his mouth like acid.

Ursula looked into his eyes, they looked cold and angry, she had never seen him like this. For a moment she felt frightened of him and his strength, her chest tightened. Did she really know him as well as she thought? After all, he had only been employed here for about six months. Did she really know what he was capable of? No she mustn't think like that, she was being silly, it's no wonder with her husband lying dead on the terrace. Walters loved her, he'd do anything for her.

Walters relaxed his grip and pulled her into his chest. He couldn't bear that she might be afraid of him. "I'm sorry, I've frightened you. It's only because I love you and I want to protect you. It's going to be alright, Ursula, I promise." He meant every word. He hadn't known this woman long but she had gotten under his skin, into his heart. The Colonel had pushed her too far, whatever she'd done he would do anything in his power to protect her.

She let herself relax and sank into him, she could feel his heart beating. His arms around her were now gentle and loving, she felt safe. She had been crazy to think he could be a danger to her. She thought about the glass she had taken from the Colonel, now washed and back behind the bar. She would do anything to protect him. They had a chance of a good life together now the Colonel was gone. Stupid, stupid doctor. Why didn't he just sign the death certificate? She could feel her panic rising again and couldn't stop her mind from leaping from scenario to scenario.

Walters feeling her tense again pushed her away slightly. "Hey, come on, it's going to be alright. Take deep breaths, that's better. You need to stay calm, we don't want the police seeing you like this."

As her breathing slowed she moved away from him and tried to calm her jagged nerves. They just had to get through the next few hours. There was a muted conversation outside her door, she nodded to Walters and he opened it. They caught the backs of the doctor and a uniformed policeman going down the hall towards the sitting room. When they had disappeared down the hall, Ursula quickly opened the door wider, slipped through and went up the stairs to her room, leaving Walters staring up at her.

Plain & Purl, Blocks & Patterns

Jazz summoned once again by the bell stopped before she reached the reception desk, thrown at the amount of police there were pouring through the door. One of them in civilian clothes stepped forward.

"Good morning. I'm Detective Chief Inspector Carley, where is the deceased?" He held out his warrant card to Jazz.

Jazz stood frozen to the spot and could barely breathe the words out. "On the terrace, go down the hall, turn right into the sitting room and through the French doors."

The detective directed his SOCO team to carry on, they were already geared up and suited in their hooded protective clothing. They pushed past Jazz on their way to the terrace.

Carley smiled at the girl who was understandably nervous. "What's your name?"

"Jazz."

Well Jazz, can you tell me where I can find Mrs Jeffries, the deceased's wife?"

Jazz, nervous and flustered, tried to pull herself together. "I believe she's in her bedroom, shall I call her?"

"Please, is that her office back there," He indicated to the room behind the reception counter.

"Yes."

"Then ask her to wait for me in there please." Carley tapped his fingers on the counter, eager to get on.

Jazz picked up the telephone on the desk and pressed the button for Mrs Jeffries bedroom. "I'm sorry to disturb you Mrs Jeffries but the police are here and he says can you wait in your office. She says she will be right down."

"Good, now where are the rest of the staff and guests?" He asked.

"Most of the guests and all the staff except me are in the kitchen finishing breakfast." Jazz replied.

"Most ? Where are the others?"

"There are two ladies eating breakfast in the dining room." Jazz replied.

"What's your name?"

"Jazz."

"Well Jazz, would you mind going and telling the ladies to join the others in the kitchen? You are all to stay there until I say you can leave."

Jazz hesitated, her heart sank at the thought of having to try and move Josie, "I don't think that old ba.." She started again. "I'm not sure one of the ladies in the dining room will listen to me. I don't think I will be able to get her into the kitchen, she's like a bit difficult."

"Oh, difficult is she? I like difficult. Show me the way, it's probably a good idea to introduce myself to everybody anyway."

Jazz led the detective to the dining room where Josie and Mary were eating their breakfast

"Ladies. I'm afraid you are going to have to take your breakfast into the kitchen." He looked at Jazz, "you carry their plates and they can carry their tea. Come along ladies out."

"I don't think so. I've paid a lot of money to stay here. It's already been a very distressing morning for me and I'm not having my breakfast disturbed any further. So you young man must wait until I have finished." Josie took a mouthful of sausage and egg.

"Ma'am you have a choice. You can either take your breakfast with you or you can leave your breakfast here but either way you will make your way to the kitchen now."

"Well, who do you think you are ordering me about?" Josie protested.

"I'm the police. Detective Chief Inspector Carley. It won't be for long, so come along, don't make a fuss."

"What nonsense is this?" Josie said.

"Oh for goodness sake Josie, shut up. For once in your life do what someone has asked you to do." Mary picked up her breakfast and her cup and saucer and marched out of the room.

Jazz wanted to applaud, at Mary's brave outburst. Instead she reached over and plucked Josie's breakfast and cup and saucer from under her nose and followed Mary out the door.

"Ma'am?" The detective said.

Josie, shocked at Mary's unexpected revolt, stood up, picked up her handbag and followed Jazz out the door, a very cross look on her face.

The detective stopped in the doorway of the kitchen and clapped his hands. "If I could have your attention please. My name is Detective Chief Inspector Carley. As you are all aware a death has occurred here this morning requiring a police presence. There is nothing to worry about as it is standard procedure in an unexpected death. I need you all to remain in here as we may need to take statements from you all. We'll try to be as quick as possible so as not to interrupt your day any further. One of my men will come and fetch you if and when we're ready for you. Thank you for your cooperation." He turned and shut the door behind him, ignoring all the questions fired at him from the guests. He turned to the constable who would be guarding the kitchen, "I didn't realise there were so many of them. DS Flower should be here any minute then we can start taking witness statements. Give the station a quick call and see if D S Perrot is in, ask him to come out here. Otherwise we'll be here all day and it's not as if we know if all this is necessary yet but better safe than sorry."

"Yes sir, will do." The constable took a few steps down the hallway to make the call. Carley carried on walking back to the reception area where Mrs Jeffries was waiting for him. He introduced himself, offered his condolences and explained the reason for the police being called in. He then asked her to go to the kitchen and stay with the other guests until she was called.

Plain & Purl All-Over Patterns

Carley had already pulled his protective suit on, he added a mask and pulled on a pair of latex gloves and some plastic shoe protectors. Carefully he walked across the sterile stepping mats laid out to protect any evidence across the terrace. He was pleased to find that his team had been busy and the scene was protected. They wouldn't normally have a SOCO team available here in North Devon, it was very rare for there to be a murder. But it just so happened that a SOCO team were in the area on team building exercises and the course tutor was with Carley when the call came in and he jumped at the chance for some on the job training. As well as not usually having the resources available Carley wouldn't expect to come out for a domestic death. However the GP had expressed serious concerns in his initial phone call. Carley didn't want to take any chances if it turned out to be something more. Trouble was it was probably too late for any ground evidence. Goodness knows how many of the guests and staff had trampled over the crime scene if it was a crime scene. The whole area was now marked with numbers where possible evidence had been found and removed for inspection later. The SOCO team were taking their last pictures and walking away as he joined the

Forensic Pathologist Simon Green who stood waiting for him next to the body.

"Morning Carley, odd one this."

"Morning Simon, what have we got then?" He put an extra strong mint in his mouth, it helped a bit with the smell.

"I'm not sure. There is nothing that is smacking me in the face like a wet kipper but I agree with the chap's GP, it smells a bit fishy."

Carley, used to the pathologist's humour leaned in closer, studying the corpse.

"There are no facial contortions." Carley said.

"No, there is some swelling and some dried blood in his nose cavity but no dried substance around his mouth or any obvious outward signs of an injury that could cause death." The pathologist said

"It is strange." Carley said.

"Take a look at his fingers." The pathologist lifted one hand and showed Carley the burn marks. "He was smoking a cigar at the time of his death, we've bagged it for evidence. If he was only asleep this would have woken him up toots sweet."

"So he was already dead when the cigar burned down."

"As a dodo. He'd been hitting the bottle. There is a strong smell of alcohol but you will note, no sign of a glass or a bottle."

"So what are your initial thoughts? Any idea of the time of death?" Carley asked.

"You are like the early bird after the first worm, Carley. I'll know more when I get him back to the lab because at the moment it looks like natural causes. But I had a chat with his GP, he's no fool and he saw the deceased less than a week ago and apparently he was as fit as a butcher's dog. The deceased was renewing his prescription for Viagra and had a thorough health check. Something here made the GP's nose twitch and it's that same something that's making my bottom itch." He turned to the men waiting with the stretcher and body bag. "Speed bonny boat chaps, the cargo's waiting." The pathologist said.

Leaving the men to remove the body, he and Carley walked across to the other side of the terrace.

"Look Simon, I know you are going to tell me that you are up to your eyes in it but can you tell me when you are going to be able to do the initial examination? I need some answers on this one pretty quick before these guests scatter to the four corners of England."

"Right as usual Sherlock. Chock-o-block. I've an idiot who jumped off a cliff tombstoning at Parracombe and an RTA. Bloody holiday traffic, they drive on our country lanes like they're still on the M25. But they'll keep. I'm intrigued with this case. If I can't find anything with my initial examination, we will probably be relying on toxicology. I think it's likely we'll need an autopsy. I'll get on to it as soon as I'm back."

" Thanks Simon."

"Nice place this I might bring Felicity here for a weekend, she does love a garden. Toodle Pip" Simon put his hand up in the air and waggled his fingers.

Fancy Knitting

DI Carley met DS Sonya Flower at the reception desk. "Ah you've arrived at the perfect time, morning Sonya. I've called in DS Davey Perrott too, I've left instructions for him to start interviewing some of the other guests. I hope I didn't call you away from something important but I need your special skills this morning."

"Morning sir, no you've saved me from the Super's latest equality ideas meeting." DS Flower replied with a wry smile.

"Oh Lord, what's he thinking of now?"

" He sent me a list of things he thought could be implemented to make us 'girls' feel more comfortable. I was supposed to add my suggestions and meet with him this morning to discuss."

"Then I've saved you and him from a world of embarrassment and tears, mostly his." Carley laughed.

"Too right sir but sadly it's only postponed. Now what do we have here?" She whipped out her iPad ready to take notes.

He was still a notebook and pen man, he could see the benefits of tablets but he wasn't confident enough to rely on them. Luckily for him his DS's were more than capable and it was a quick method of printing out statements etc. "I'm not quite sure at the moment but this is the story so far. The owners of the house are a Colonel and a Mrs Jeffries. The Colonel was found dead this morning on the outside terrace from a suspected heart attack. However the deceased's own GP wasn't happy as the death was completely unexpected. He had seen the Colonel only last week apparently and he found him as fit as a butcher's dog in his words. The Forensic Pathologist could find no noticeable injuries on the body except for severe burns to the fingers of one hand. He'll be looking for poisons but there was no visible sign of that on the deceased's face, no residue powder, rash or burns and no odour. It looked like a peaceful death as if he had fallen asleep." Carley said.

"Sir, when he didn't come to bed, why didn't his wife go and look for him? " She asked.

"I don't know yet, but we shall soon find out. On paper there isn't anything that jumps out at me but my gut tells me this might not be a straightforward death by natural causes."

"Are you sure that's not because you missed your breakfast?" She said with a grin.

"Mmn, could be, I'm finding early mornings harder these days. So we have a lot of questions to ask a lot of people. We'll set ourselves up in the owner's office and we'll speak to the widow first but before that I want to say a few words to them all and introduce you as you'll be doing some of the interviews. He led the way down the hallway to the kitchen, talking as they went. Prepare yourself, there is at least one awkward customer."

"Isn't there always?" She laughed following him.

The constable guarding the kitchen door stood aside as they entered.

The Inspector had a few words with him then opened the door, immediately the chatter died.

"Morning again everyone as I've already said, my name is Detective Inspector Carley, this is Detective Sergeant Flower and she will be interviewing some of you as well." There were a few sniggers.

"Before any comedian says anything, I've heard them all before." She said, catching one of the culprit's eyes and cocking an eyebrow.

"Thank you for your patience. At least it looks and smells like you have all enjoyed a hearty breakfast." Carley smiled. " Let me reassure you this is purely a routine matter in a case of an unexpected death. We are going to ask you all to provide a statement for the last twenty four hours. We will be as quick as we can so as not to inconvenience you. We will see you one at a time then after that you can go to your rooms or anywhere in the gardens as long as you don't leave the premises until I say so." Carley informed them.

"I've never heard of anything so ridiculous. What on earth do we have to be interrogated for? My sister and I are taking up Mrs Jeffries offer of a full refund and leaving here as soon as we can organise a taxi." Josie said, putting her teacup down so hard it threatened to break the saucer.

"Crafty Mare, old Ursula offered a partial refund," whispered Tony.

"Ma'am in cases of unexpected deaths..." Carley didn't get very far in his explanation before he was interrupted.

"Clearly the odious little man drank himself to death. Come Mary, we're leaving" She stood up from her chair.

The others were shocked at her comment about the Colonel, especially right in front of his widow.

D S Flower, reached behind for her handcuffs and walked towards Josie holding them out. "Let me assist you ma'am."

Mary sat back down in alarm but Josie stayed standing defiantly.

"We have a nice holding cell back at the police station for you. Of course it's not as nice as waiting in here to give your statement but your choice." DS Flower held out the handcuffs and stared at Josie.

Tony giggled, "Cor she's hard core."

The others were struggling to keep straight faces, even the Inspector had a twitch at the side of his mouth. Josie, obviously furious but powerless against the situation she found herself in, sat down. "I shall be complaining to your superior."

"Please do. He's over there." She nodded to the Inspector but she wasn't finished with Josie. She tucked her handcuffs back in the rear pocket of her trousers and pulled out her tablet. "What is your name Ma'am?"

"Why do you want my name?" Josie's voice had lost some of its bravado and she looked a little nervous.

"I like to keep track of people who are looking to escape from the scene of a possible crime," D S Flower said.

Mary decided that she had better save her sister from any further embarrassment. "Sergeant, I think my sister understands the seriousness of the situation and I'm sure she doesn't want to upset Mrs Jeffries who has just lost her husband. So we will sit here and quietly wait like everybody else."

May couldn't help herself. "Go Mary."

Josie gave May one of her evil looks but she ignored it and smiled sweetly back at her.

"I know it's tempting and probably too late but please don't discuss the Colonel's death between yourselves until after we have your record of events. We want your statements to be as accurate as possible and we don't want them muddled with other peoples. We will try not to keep you too long. Mrs Jeffries, can I ask you to come along first?" Carley requested.

Looking pale but composed Mrs Jeffries quickly flashed a look at Walters then got up from her chair. "Would you care for a tea or coffee Inspector?"

"As I missed breakfast, that would be very much appreciated. Tea please for both of us." Carley replied.

Mrs Jeffries looked across at Nancy who was now sitting at the table with her eyes closed and her head resting on her crossed arms. When she didn't move she looked across the kitchen and asked, "Walters, would you be so kind as to make up a tray of tea and biscuits for the Detectives please and bring it to the office."

"Of course."

Carley looked at Walters and said. "Pass the tray to the constable outside the door Mr Walters and he'll bring it along. Thank you." He opened the door and let Mrs Jeffries through. DS Flower spent a few seconds giving Josie a hard stare before following them.

Forming Scallops

Carley watched the woman in front of him. She was clearly nervous and upset but there were no obvious signs of grief. "Mrs Jeffries, first my condolences on the death of your husband, it must have been a terrible shock for you. I believe your husband's GP explained that we are called in when a death is unexpected or unexplained. I need to ask you a few questions, it is purely routine and if you need a break, let me know."

"Yes I understand but surely there is no need for all this." She swept her arm to include DS Flower who had tucked herself in a corner on a seat behind Carley ready to take notes. "My poor guests feel like criminals. I'm going to get the most dreadful reviews and it will badly affect my fledgling business."

Carley ignored her speech and carried on. "Tell me how many people live here Mrs Jeffries apart from you and your husband."

"Well there is Walters, he's my right-hand man, he helps run the business and acts as a sort of butler when we have guests. Nancy our chef and Jazz our waitress and chambermaid. They are the full time employees and I have a cleaning woman a Mrs Hattersley who comes in the mornings, only she's not here this morning. Walters, rang her and put her off. Then I have two gardeners James Norris and Dick Dalberty who tend the gardens and run our small nursery."

"Thank you. Can you talk me through your day yesterday starting from breakfast and please don't leave anything out however insignificant?"

Mrs Jeffries gave a big sigh as if to say what a waste of time but talked through her Tuesday, finishing with dinner in the evening.

"What did you do after dinner?" Carley asked, watching her face closely.

"I went to the office to prepare for the next day's excursion. This morning I was going to give the guests a guided tour of the gardens and then a talk on the history of the house. When I finished my preparations I went straight to bed."

"Alone?" Carley asked.

"Yes of course alone." Mrs Jeffries replied, pasting a neutral expression on her face attempting to hide her inner nervousness. She was used to hiding her feelings, there had been plenty of practice on the many social occasions she'd had to put up with her husband's embarrassing behaviour.

"What time was that?"

"Sorry?" Thinking about the times her husband had embarrassed her, she had missed what the detective was saying.

"What time did you go to bed?" Carley repeated.

"About ten."

"Your husband didn't go to bed with you?" Carley asked.

"No."

"Weren't you worried when he didn't come to bed?"

"My husband and I have separate bedrooms, I'm a light sleeper and he likes to stay up late."

"Did you speak to him at all after dinner?"

There was a slight hesitation before she answered, "No. What is this all about Inspector? Surely my husband died from a heart attack. I don't understand what's going on here, treating me and my guests like murderers. Is it really necessary to lock them in the kitchen and interrogate them like this?" Clearly angry, two bright spots of colour appeared on her cheeks, stark against her pale complexion.

Carley decided not to push any further even though he was sure she wasn't telling him all the truth. "Thank you, that will be all for now. As I've already explained, until we can establish how your husband died we must follow procedure. Please stay on the premises for the time being, that goes for everyone staying here. Be assured we will tread carefully with your guests."

"Do I have to stay in the kitchen?" She asked.

"No. You can stay in the house or grounds for the time being, you can go anywhere you want except for the kitchen or terrace for now."

"Can I take the file with my notes and information on this morning's talk please?" Mrs Jeffries asked.

"Yes of course, just let my DS cast her eyes over it."

Mrs Jeffries looked at him as she rose, "is that really necessary?"

"Purely procedure Ma'am," DS Flower stood, laid her tablet down on the table and moved to the filing cabinet with Mrs Jeffries.

Mrs Jeffries pulled out the relevant file, his DS looked through it and finding nothing suspicious nodded her approval to Carley.

"Cut along and fetch the chef please Sonya."

DS Flower was following Mrs Jeffries towards the door but stopped as she turned at the door. "Inspector, don't believe everything that woman tells you. She is under the illusion that my husband was in love with her. The only person my husband loved was himself." She turned and left.

Carley put his hand up to his DS and said, "stop, close the door. Well, I wasn't expecting that. What did you think of her?"

"She's not exactly the grieving widow is she? And she was

definitely lying when you asked if she had seen her husband after dinner."

"That's what I thought."

"Let's see if any of the staff spill the beans on what's been going on."

DS Flower returned to the office, opening the door for Nancy who was carrying a tray with cups, saucers, milk jug sugar, teapot and a plate of lemon biscuits. She placed it on the desk then sat on the chair by the desk. DS Flower slipped back in her corner, tablet at the ready.

Carley assessed the woman in front of him. Mid-forties, stocky build, dark mousy hair poking out from her chef's cap and round face with plain features, her nose and eyes red from weeping. "Hello Nancy, clearly you are very upset and who wouldn't be after the experience you've had this morning. Can you tell us what happened from when you first arrived today? "

"I live here, I have two rooms in the attic and that's not as bad as it sounds. They've been done up from when they used to be servants quarters."

"Does Walters have rooms up there too?" Carley asked.

"Yes. Not that he's ever in there much."

Carley left that pulled thread, saving it to unravel later. "So back to this morning."

"I got down to the kitchen at about seven, a bit earlier than usual, it's hard to sleep these light mornings. I put the kettle on to make myself a cup of tea, then I went out of the back door to fetch some herbs for breakfast. I have a little raised bed in the kitchen garden outside the back door. As I straightened up from picking I looked across the gardens as I usually do and then across to the terrace, where I saw." She couldn't speak as the tears came.

"It's okay, take your time." Carley said kindly.

After a few minutes she composed herself, wiping her eyes and blowing her nose.

"Are you alright to carry on?" Carley said.

"Yes." She took a deep shuddering breath. "I could see the Colonel sitting in a chair at the far side of the terrace. I knew straight away something was wrong. He's never up that early and he was wearing the same suit as yesterday which was really odd."

DS Flower looked up and glanced at Nancy but didn't interrupt.

I dropped the herbs and walked over. As I got nearer I thought he must have fallen asleep and been out here all night. But when I was close I could see that he was dead. I touched his hand to make sure but it was cold and." She buried her face in her hands and sobbed.

Carley waited until she had composed herself again. "What happened then Nancy?"

"It's all a bit of a blur but I think I must have screamed, then one of the guests arrived and another one took me over to sit down away from the." She didn't finish her sentence.

"How long have you worked here Nancy? Can you tell me a little bit about the Colonel and his wife?" Carley asked.

"I came here about a month after the Colonel, about eight months ago. I used to work at the golf club and I met the Colonel there. He was always very complimentary about my food and when he married her, he asked me if I would come and work for him."

No love lost there with Mrs Jeffries, Carley thought. "Bit of a change for you going from a busy Golf clubhouse to a small country house that wasn't yet opened for guests. What made you decide to come here?"

Nancy blushed, her face mottled red. I came because he asked me to, I wanted to be near him. The Colonel didn't want to open the house as a hotel; it was her idea but I said to him this could be a real chance for me to run my own kitchen in a small boutique hotel. I wanted to make a name for myself as a country house chef."

What can you tell me about the Colonel and Mrs Jeffries relationship?"

Nancy sneered. "There wasn't one. The way that woman treated that darling man was abominable. Separate rooms after a month of marriage. When he's married to me there won't be any separation..." She stopped, her hand flew to her mouth in horror when she realised what she'd said.

"Carry on Nancy, you can tell us." Carley said then waited, he'd found in his experience that witnesses would often feel uncomfortable and eager to fill the silence. He could hear a fly buzzing at the window, he leant back in his chair.

Nancy sat up in her chair. "Well alright, I'll tell you. He was going to divorce that woman and marry me. We were going to make this place a success and I was going to get a Michelin star." Her voice faded as the reality hit her. "I can't believe he's gone. She never even shed a tear, the cold-hearted bitch. She's too loved up with that tall streak of sneaky. Do Ya know where he spends his nights? In her ladyship's bedroom, not his own attic room. She thinks we don't know but we do, everyone does. Walters was going to be named in the divorce, this hotel was going to be mine. She doesn't deserve it." She dabbed at her tears.

"Where were you after dinner last night Nancy?" Carley asked, changing the subject.

"After I'd cleared up and had my own dinner I went up to my sitting room and watched telly."

"Did you see the Colonel at all after dinner?"

"No. Can I go now, I need to get on with my baking and cooking."

"Yes but don't speak to anyone else in the kitchen and don't leave the premises. Can you tell the constable to send in one of the other guests please when you get back to the kitchen?"

Some Interesting Textures

The guests had all been called one after the other from the kitchen until there was only Tony and May left. The constable poked his head around the door of the kitchen and asked Tony to go to Ursula's office, then he asked May to follow him. She trailed after him down the hall when he stopped and held the dining room door open for her.

"Miss May Wood sir." The constable said.

"Davey! I hardly recognised you at first, I don't think I've ever seen you with your clothes on." May covered her mouth with her hand instantly wishing she had an inner filter that could have stopped those words, she could hear the constable chuckling as he closed the door.

"Well that's going to cause a bit of gossip down the station, thanks for that."

"Davey, I am so sorry. It didn't cross my mind that it might be you who would interview me, I couldn't believe who I was seeing. Although I suppose I shouldn't be surprised, I know you are a policeman."

"Too late now, don't worry but it's Detective Sergeant Perrot." He smiled at her and held her gaze for a few moments too long.

May gazed at him, boy did he look good, he wore a dark blue suit that fitted like the proverbial glove, a crisp white shirt and a snazzy tie. His eyes were a dark brown and his hair, usually a sweaty mess, was neatly combed. May had the unexpected desire to run her fingers through it and muss it up. Faggots and gin he was gorgeous, she could feel the heat rising in her body in response. That had never happened before and she had often seen him when he was half-naked in Trudy's place. Then she remembered their midnight encounter.

"May?"

May jerked back into the room as she realised Davey or DS Perrott as she had to think of him, had been talking to her. "Sorry I was miles away, what did you say?"

"I was saying that although we know each other this interview will have to be conducted in a professional manner, I'm sure you understand."

"Yes, of course, you're completely lovely, a policeman, I mean you're right, um."

DS Perrott smiled. "Relax May, I need to take a few details down and then you can tell me your version of the events."

After giving all her personal details, May went through the previous evening and then the moment she heard Nancy scream.

"Can you describe the scene when you arrived and try to remember every little thing, it might be important?" DS Perrott asked.

"It was really scary and shocking to find the Colonel dead and to see Nancy hanging on to him weeping and wailing. He was clearly dead but I couldn't see any obvious injuries, it looked like he had just fallen asleep. It sounds odd but I think he was still wearing his suit from last night. There was an empty glass resting on his thigh and a whisky decanter on the table next to him but something else that was strange is that after all the kerfuffle and there was just me and Mrs Jeffries on the terrace, the decanter disappeared. I can't think of anything else."

"Thank you, that's all very helpful. I'm sure it will turn out to be natural causes but we have to make an initial investigation just in case. I'm really sorry about this May. I hope it doesn't spoil your holiday. Trudy told me you wanted to get away for a bit to relax and recharge your batteries, try and enjoy the rest of your week."

She flushed embarrassed at the thought that he knew the reason for her wanting to get away.

He stood and walked around the table, as she rose from the chair he placed his hand in the small of her back and guided her towards the door. Reaching in front of her to open it he guided her through and she turned to thank him finding herself mere inches away. The words wouldn't come, she felt breathless as their gaze locked, he broke away first turning and walking away down the hall.

Sir Humphrey Repton 1752 - 1818

May looked out of her window down the garden towards the river below and mused on her interview with Davey or as she must get used to calling him DS Perrot. I can't understand why I had never seen him before, well of course I've seen him before but not in the way I saw him this morning. God I hope I didn't make a fool of myself, was he aware of the effect he was having on me? I can still feel where his hand rested on my back and there was that moment when we looked into each other's eyes. There was definitely a spark of attraction, I know I didn't imagine it. Oh for goodness sake, I'm acting like a love-struck teenager. I don't imagine for one minute he would be interested in me. He's way out of my league, good looking, the body of a Greek God, kind, health freak. He probably goes for stick-thin lollipop head Blondes and I'm definitely a curvy-figured brunette. She turned away from the window and went downstairs to join the others.

Although all of the police paraphernalia had been removed and the area cleaned, Ursula felt it would be rather uncomfortable for everyone to gather on the terrace. There wasn't time now for a tour of the garden so she had asked the guests to meet her in the library but she was a few minutes late.

"Sorry to have kept you waiting. There were a few pressing matters requiring my attention."

"I'd have thought after the shocking morning and distress you've caused us you would have least made an effort to be on time." Josie said, striding up to Ursula and folding her arms.

There were gasps from the others, this was totally uncalled for and low even coming from Josie.

Ursula was speechless at this unexpected attack and couldn't stop the tears forming. May slipped her arm through Ursulas' and steered her passed Josie. "So Ursula, tell us more about Humphrey Repton who designed these gardens."

The garden talk went well and everyone was fascinated with the famous Moroccan bound red book containing Humphrey Repton's watercolour illustrations of the garden design, something he did for every garden he designed. They thanked Ursula for the talk and then gathered on the terrace for lunch. May couldn't help her eyes travelling to where the Colonel had been sitting but there wasn't a chair or table there anymore. They had all been moved and rearranged in a different area of the garden. May was relieved she hadn't fancied sitting there and was sure the others would feel the same.

Heel Flap

After another delicious lunch and a bathroom break the guests had settled down on their respective tables and taken their knitting out. Their homework had been to knit up to where the heel will begin. Ivy arrived with another plastic box, May hoped it contained some more yarn as she just loved to feel and squish the different colour yarns; she knew she wouldn't be able to resist buying more.

"Good afternoon everyone. First of all I would like to say how very sorry I am for the loss of the Colonel and it must have been very upsetting for you all. Ursula has asked me to carry on as per your wishes. So I think we should put it out of our minds for this afternoon and enjoy this lovely weather and move on with knitting our socks. This afternoon is going to be exciting as we are all going to start on our heels."

"Sounds like we're going to do some line-dancing," Alice said with a chuckle.

"Don't look so scared Tony, I can promise you we will all manage it and enjoy it. Tomorrow is even more exciting when we learn how to turn the heel, it's magical." Ivy smiled around the group.

"I wish she'd stop treating us like children." Josie hissed.

Ivy sensibly ignored her and carried on. "Before we start on our heel flap journey I want to mention what will be a dirty word to some of you in this sunny month of June," she paused, "Christmas."

There was a collective gasp and a few laughs from the knitters.

"Us knitters know we need to start our Christmas knitting projects early in order to have our gifts ready by December twenty fourth. I started knitting my Christmas present socks back in February." She lifted the lid off the box by her side and pulled out several Christmassy coloured yarns in reds and greens, some with a lustre in them that sparkled in the sun and several packets of Christmas sock kits. There was a murmur of excitement from the knitters.

"You are going to love these, they are gorgeous aren't they, I can see by some of your faces you are dying..." Ivy paused, her face flushed as she realised her gaffe. "I mean you can't wait to come and take a closer look at these. Some of these knit up in stripes and some in patterns. You can even knit them in two different colours like these green and red. They will knit up like elf-socks, aren't they great fun?" She picked up two more balls, these have a sparkle to them. This midnight blue knits up like a winter night's sky full of stars and this one like a sparkly Christmas garland." Ivy then held up two colourful packets. "These Christmas packs are great value, they contain a book of knitting patterns for hats, scarfs and sock patterns. They are a little more challenging than the basic sock pattern we've knitted. They also have four 100 gram balls of yarn all in Christmassy colours. At the end of our session this afternoon you are welcome to come and take a look. I have enough stock of all of them should you wish to buy any of the yarns here."

. . .

"That's a cheap trick to get us to spend more money with her." Josie said loud enough for everyone to hear.

Ivy, flushed with embarrassment and didn't know what to say for a moment.

"Thank you for bringing them and showing us Ivy. I know by the time it was closer to Christmas and they start offering these yarns it would be too late for me to knit them in time to give as presents. It makes sense to start knitting them now. I didn't even know there were special Christmas coloured yarns. They look scrummy and it certainly saves me from having to hunt them down."

Ivy felt very grateful to May for coming to her rescue, she was such a kind person. I shall pop something extra in her bag if she buys yarn this afternoon. "Now I just want to show you these, they are a trio of needles that I personally find extremely useful for knitting the heel flap, picking up stitches for the gusset and for decreasing for the toes. Please don't feel I am trying to sell you more things for my sake, these are expensive but well worth it as they make knitting socks easier. I'm going to come around and hand out spare double ended needles to everyone."

May put her hand up, "Excuse me Ivy can you bring me some of those trio needles please and I'll pay you at the end of the session?"

Several of the others called out for some too.

"Ok, I'll bring both around to each table." Ivy made her way around distributing needles then went back to her table."

"Right, let's go for those heels."

Ivy went on to demonstrate how to knit the heel flap on her own sock and then worked with each of them individually, constantly moving around to check their progress. They all had a chuckle when she discovered Tony had slipped his purl stitches as well his knit stitches, creating a tight flap. Ivy assured him it was a common mistake and he laughed along with everyone else. Ivy told them of the time she had managed to knit two heels on one sock when she had been knitting whilst engrossed in an exciting film.

May was thrilled with the way her sock was coming along and was really enjoying the process. She loved the little short needles that meant she could just keep knitting around the sock, the four needles that Evelyn was knitting with looked far too complicated for her. When they stopped at the end of the session. She went a bit yarn crazy and bought one of the Christmas knitting kits and a ball each of the two sparkly yarns, one a midnight blue the other that knitted up like a Christmas garland. She couldn't wait to start knitting with them and knew Trudy was going to love the sparkly blue pair she planned to knit her for Christmas; she could wear them with her short ankle high heeled boots in the winter. They had all gathered around Ivy's table chatting about the luscious yarns, all except for Josie. She hadn't bought any of the Christmas yarns and had left the terrace after a few cross words with her sister Mary who wanted to stay and chat with the others.

"Why don't we form a Socks-Chat group on our phones, then we can keep in touch, share our progress and pics of our socks?" May suggested then could have bitten her tongue as she remembered that Lucy didn't have a phone and Mary probably didn't either. She rested her hand on Lucy's arm. "What an idiot, sorry Lucy I forgot you didn't have a phone."

"That's okay May, don't worry. It's a great idea." She laughed. "One of the first things I am going to do when I get home is buy a phone, an Ipad, a television and get on the internet. I use a computer at the library and I'm very confident with them, it's silly not to have one of my own. I've been wallowing around changing nothing since my mother died, it's time I lived my own life now. I might need a bit of help though." Lucy looked at May, she really liked her and hoped that they could become friends.

"We don't live far from each other, so we could meet up and

go shopping for them, I love a good shop." May said, giving Lucy a shoulder bump.

They all pulled out their phones and swapped numbers. May was pleased to see that Mary had a phone, she didn't know why she had thought she wouldn't. She expected it was because Josie seemed so mean and controlling of Mary.

Mary noted May's expression. "Surprised? I don't live with Josie you know and if you were to see me in the supermarket I'd look like every other woman there. I'm not as old fashioned as her and I don't do everything she tells me. Sadly Josie has fallen out with all of our family and doesn't speak to any of them. I have two sons and three grandchildren and like to keep in touch with them. I'm sorry for Josie, she can't seem to help herself and her attitude alienates most people. Not one person in her knitting circle would come on this holiday with her and I felt sorry for her, which is why I'm here."

"Well I'm very glad you did Mary," Ivy said. She packed up her things, said her goodbyes and left.

After everyone had finished swapping telephone numbers they all left leaving Tony, Michael, May and Lucy on the terrace.

Zigzag Patterns

Tony nipped inside to order another round of tea, then they all settled down for a good gossip. This was the first opportunity they'd had to discuss the morning's events without the others overhearing.

"I couldn't believe my eyes and ears this morning," Tony said. "Fancy, Nancy and the Colonel?"

The others all burst out laughing and couldn't stop.

"Fancy Nancy," May said, looking at a bemused Tony and struggling to get the words out through her laughter.

It was a while before they could compose themselves.

"I know this is really bad of us but oh boy does it feel good, I think we all needed a good laugh after this morning." May said.

"I still feel a bit guilty though," Lucy said.

"Why should you feel guilty, you didn't kill the Colonel did you?" Michael asked.

That set them off again, May had tears streaming down her face.

"Oh stop it. Enough," Lucy said, holding her stomach.

Jazz arrived with their tea at that moment.

"Glad you're all having a good time and that bastard popping his clogs didn't upset you. You're all lovely people, he doesn't deserve any of your sympathy. There we are a pot of tea for three and a pot of decaf for one. I've sneaked a few of Nancy's shortbread biscuits to keep you going till dinner. I'm off now to see to Nan, I'll see you this evening." Before anyone could answer her, Jazz was off across the terrace and through the door to the kitchen.

"No love lost there then with Jazz and the Colonel. I bet the poor girl has had to dodge and fend off the lecherous creep." Tony said.

"What a lovely girl she is caring for her nan whilst having to work for a living, that must be hard." May said.

"I only hope that her nan appreciates everything that she does for her." Lucy said.

Poor Lucy, May thought her mother must have been a really difficult woman.

"She's a real sweetheart," Tony agreed.

"Is it just me? Or did you notice that Ursula didn't share a tear over the Colonel." May asked.

"Not a grieving Widow, that's for sure." Tony said.

"Do you think Ursula is having an affair with Walters like Nancy said?" Lucy asked.

"Duh, haven't you been watching them? They are clearly together, I would say they are in luurve." Michael said, in a Barry White voice.

That set them off laughing again.

"Goodness if we can't contain ourselves whilst just drinking tea, what are we going to be like after a couple of drinks tonight? May said.

"Oh you are such a romantic," Tony said, nudging Michael with his shoulder.

"No, I think Michael is right, I believe they are in love. You can see the way he looks at her and this morning when we discovered the Colonel. They arrived together and he was glued to her side even though we were all watching ." May said

"Yes but that may be because they work closely together and he was supporting a friend." Lucy said.

"Friend? I think that's a friend with benefits. Didn't you notice that they both arrived together in their dressing gowns but Ursula had Walters' belt and Walters had Ursula's belt?" May said.

"Wow, you're very observant aren't you?" Michael pointed out.

"I'm a teaching assistant, I have to be observant. My students say I have eyes in the back of my head." May said.

They finished their tea and after chatting for a further half an hour, they packed up their knitting and left for their rooms.

Pressing Knitted Fabric

The guests gathered in the sitting room for drinks before dinner and after Walters had served them from the bar, Ursula addressed them.

"Thank you all for your patience this morning and I am truly sorry that you had to endure police interviews. That was certainly not on the itinerary for this sock knitting retreat which was meant to be relaxing and enjoyable."

"We should be given compensation for all the distress." Josie interrupted.

Ignoring her, Ursula continued. "I'm glad to say that the police have finished their investigation and confirmed the Colonel died from natural causes. I would like you to put all this unpleasantness behind you and enjoy the rest of your stay. There will be complimentary wine with dinner. I hope you will excuse me but I will not be eating with you this evening. I hope you all understand." Ursula, with a slight dip of her head, gracefully left the room.

After dinner they were all getting up from the table when Josie started arguing with Mary and belittling her. May lost her temper, she knew she shouldn't interfere but she couldn't bear bullies. She couldn't stand by and watch Josie bully Mary and she was fed up with Josie and the poisonous remarks she'd been sticking in, especially the ones directed at Tony and Michael. She moved to stand between the sisters, facing Josie. "Why do you have to be so nasty all the time? You are vile to everyone, even your own sister who is so kind to you and doesn't deserve to be treated so badly. If you're not careful you'll end up dying all alone with no friends or family and you will deserve it." Nobody said a word, they were surprised and a bit embarrassed at May's outburst but none of them said anything as they felt Josie deserved it.

"I have never been so insulted in all my life." Josie protested.

"Perhaps if someone had told you some home truths earlier you wouldn't be so nasty now." May said quietly, stepping away. Now her temper had cooled she was starting to feel a bit wobbly over challenging Josie. She hated conflict and wouldn't normally dare to speak to anyone like that but perhaps the events of the day had unsettled her equilibrium.

"I'm not staying here to be insulted, I'm going to my room. Come along Mary." Josie strode to the door but stopped when she realised Mary wasn't following her. "Oh, so you are choosing to side with them are you? Typical, you always were a wobbling Nelly. Fine then you keep your new friends. When I get home I shall be changing my will and you and your waste of space sons and snivelling grandchildren won't get a penny. I shall be leaving it all and my house to someone who deserves it." She spat the words out, spittle flying from her mouth, her face red with anger.

Mary pulled herself up straight and stepped towards her sister. "I think you forget Josie that the house you live in doesn't solely belong to you. I own half of it whether you acknowledge it or not. The facts are that our parents left it to us both equally. You had better start being nicer to my boys because if I die before you they will inherit my half of the house. You haven't exactly been a doting aunt, you are rude and nasty to them and you have never even met their children. Why would they let you stay in the house when they could force you to sell it and use their share of the money to benefit their own families?" Although a little calmer Mary looked equally as angry as her sister. The others stood around in stunned silence as the row between the sisters raged. Eventually Josie realised she wasn't winning the argument and tried to storm off but was stopped by Evelyn and Alice who had blocked the dining room door thinking this was the ideal time for them to tackle Josie themselves.

" You stole our knitting pattern design Josie and you are selling it as your own. You are a thief," Alice said.

"Don't think you are going to get away with it, we're going to stop you." Evelyn said.

"Get out of my way, you are both ridiculous and you can't prove a thing." Josie said, pushing her way through them to the door.

Flat Toe

After Josie left it was quiet for a moment. Mary collapsed on the nearest chair, shaking. Lucy immediately went to crouch at her side. May, still a little shaky herself, sat in the chair next to her and took her hand. Tony went off to the bar in the sitting room and came back with some brandy in a glass goblet.

"Drink this, it will help." He said gently pushing the glass into Mary's shaking hands. "You look like you could do with some too May."

"No, I'm okay. I've probably had too much wine already but another glass would help."

Michael found May's glass and topped it up.

Mary sipped at the brandy coughing a little as it hit the back of her throat. To everyone's relief the colour came back into her cheeks and her breathing started to calm down.

"I'm so sorry everyone, I don't know what came over me. I shouldn't have reacted the way I did. But when she said that about my boys my mothers protective instincts took over, I don't usually let her get to me."

"I think we all understand Mary, she pushed you over the edge. You've been very tolerant of her this week. I'm the one who should say sorry for interfering, it was none of my business. Too much wine at dinner." She took a big glug of the Rose unaware of the irony. " I Know I'm being nosy but was Josie already living in your parents house when your parents died then? Was she caring for them?" May asked.

"No. Josie has only ever cared about herself. She had her own house, one that she had inherited from our aunt but even that is a bit suspect."

"Oh why was that?" May asked.

"None of the family ever saw our Aunt's will. Josie dealt with everything and stupidly we trusted her. At the time she didn't own her own house. She has always been involved with her local church and she was renting a Church owned flat. That changed after aunt died; she soon moved herself into auntie's house which was a large Victorian house in Ilfracombe. Then our mother died followed a few months later by our father and they left their house to us both. It's a huge house in Croyde and worth a small fortune. I am lucky to own my own bungalow and I'm quite comfortable there, it's near my boys and I have friends there. Our parent's house is too big for one elderly lady to live in and as Josie already had auntie's house I assumed we would sell it. I was going to use my half of the proceeds to help both my boys get on the property ladder but there was no chance of that. Without telling us Josie moved herself into our parent's house, sold auntie's house and banked herself a nice nest-egg. She's refused to sell ever since even though the house is much too big for her and will take a lot of heating, cleaning and maintenance. Anyway, enough about my problems. I apologise I shouldn't have aired our dirty linen in public." Mary said.

"Please, you have nothing to be sorry about, your sister would try a saint. Why don't you force her to sell?" May asked.

"I could take her to court but I'm afraid I can't afford the legal fees. Plus there is always the chance the court would side with her as she doesn't have anywhere else to live now she's sold her other house. It's very frustrating because if we sold her share plus what she has from auntie's house would easily buy her something more suitable." Josie replied.

"I thought she was going to leave and take the refund, how come she's still here? May asked.

"She was hoping to get a full refund but Ursula only offered a partial one, which to be honest I thought was fair. Anyway she's staying now." Mary said.

Well, we don't want it to upset the rest of our holiday so let's forget about it all now shall we and go and have more drinks on the terrace?" May patted Mary's hand and stood up.

"Great idea, I'll take a couple of bottles from the bar. I'll leave a note for Walters for when he comes to lock up later." Tony said going to the bar.

Evelyn and Alice declined more drinks and went up to their room to ring their husbands and said they wouldn't be coming back down. May slipped her arm through Marys and led the way through the French doors and onto the terrace. Tony and Michael had once again rearranged the tables so they could all sit together carefully avoiding the area where the Colonel had last been. With a bottle of red and a bottle of white wine on the table they settled down to chatter and knit the rest of the evening away.

Making Shapes With Holes

The killer smiled, it had all gone to plan. I was briefly worried when the police turned up, I wasn't expecting them. I thought the stupid GP would sign it off as a heart attack. I need to be careful not to say too much, that Inspector is no fool and his sidekick looked at me as if she could read my thoughts but I got away with it. Natural causes. The old bugger got what he deserved. I only wish it could have been a more painful death but at least this way no one suspects a thing.

Taking Care of Wools & Needles

Ursula let the water rush over her, washing away her tension and fears. She felt almost giddy with relief at the news the police had ruled the Colonel's death as a heart attack. She had thought suspicion would hang over them for days and was really surprised at how quickly the authorities had performed an autopsy. That Inspector Carley was keen and obviously had the authority to get things done. She planned to bury the Colonel as soon as it could be arranged. She'd already spoken to the funeral directors and they were collecting his body in the morning. She would be so relieved when it was all over, then she would have to decide what to do about Walters. Switching off the shower, she pulled on a towelling robe and went through to her bedroom.

Openings For Fastenings

Walters softly closed the door of Ursula's bedroom and swiftly crossed to the bed. Eyes closed she was lying back, resting on the pillows, her hair loose and slightly damp was spread out across the pillows. His heart squeezed and he thought she had never looked more beautiful. It had all been worth it. He gently laid down next to her on top of the quilt leaning on his elbow, propping his head up on his hand and gazed down upon her. Having a bit of time before he had to go and lock up after the last guests had gone to bed he'd wanted to check that Ursula was okay, it had been a hell of a day.

Hearing a sound at the door he sat up and swung his legs off the bed, careful not to wake Ursula. A folded piece of what looked like hotel stationary appeared under the door, pushed through from behind. By the time he had unlocked and opened the door whoever it was had gone. He closed the door behind him, stood in the hall and opened the note. He started to read it *'I saw what you did...'* stopped then glancing quickly at Ursula's door he headed up the stairs to his own room.

After Walters had gone, a second identical note was pushed under Ursula's door; she would find it in the morning.

Nancy was also in her room up in the attic. She was wearing faded floral cotton pyjamas and was curled up in the armchair. Her head rested on the arm of the chair, tears sliding down her face, a soggy tissue screwed up in her hand, the tv flickering in the corner. She didn't notice the note that had been pushed under her door until she got up to go to the bathroom before going to bed. She picked up the note and started to read it, '*I know what you did...*'

When Jazz had finally settled her nan comfortably in bed she went and made herself a cup of hot chocolate which she carried up to bed with her bag slung over her shoulder. She climbed into bed and rummaged around in her bag for her phone. She found it, pulled it out and a piece of hotel notepaper fluttered down and landed on her duvet.

Making Stitches

May couldn't get to sleep, the events of this morning and the image of the Colonel dead on the terrace were rolling around her brain making sleep impossible. She switched the bedside light back on, climbed out of bed and padded over to the wardrobe. After rummaging around in her suitcase, her fingers finally found what she was looking for, a notepad but after a bit more rummaging sadly no pen. Then she remembered in the dressing table drawer she'd seen some hotel stationary and a pen. After finding it she climbed back onto the bed, sitting cross-legged on top of the duvet.

Closing her eyes she thought back to this morning when she first arrived on the terrace, trying to remember as much detail as she could. Opening her eyes she started writing a list, I'm no Miss Marple but my instincts are telling me that something isn't right about the Colonel's death. Which I know is mad considering the police have ruled it a natural death but still. She started writing.

1. The Colonel was in the same chair he had been sitting in last night when they had left him on the terrace
2. His face was pale but peaceful, no visible wounds
3. Whisky glass resting between on his thigh
4. Decanter on table

5. Why didn't his wife notice he didn't come to bed?
6. Nancy was having an affair with Colonel
7. Ursula (Colonel's wife) was having an affair with Walters
8. Is there a life insurance policy on the Colonel?
9. Who wanted the Colonel dead?
10. Did Ursula want him out of the way so she could marry Walters?
11. Are there any poisons that can kill without leaving a trace? (Google it)
12. Did the police find the decanter and glass?

May re-read her notes, was she right in thinking there was possibly more to the Colonel's death than a heart attack? How could she find out? She closed the notepad and laid it down with the pen on the bedside table. Who could she talk to about her unease? It was no good talking to the Inspector, she had no actual facts to give him and he had already closed the case, he wouldn't be interested in her feelings. She'd read enough murder mysteries to know the police aren't interested in amateur sleuths interfering. Then a certain good looking detective popped into her head, there was someone who might listen to her crazy thoughts. Smiling to herself, she picked up her phone and was about to search for his number when she realised she didn't have it. Still it's probably for the best, I'm sure I'd only embarrass myself. Who am I to think I know better than the police? She dropped the phone back on the bedside table and put out the light. It was a warm night, the window was open but there was no breeze. Hot she tossed the duvet over to the empty side of the bed and spread out on the bed trying to find a cool patch. Her temperature rose higher as her thoughts strayed again to the good looking detective but in her vision he wasn't wearing his suit. He was as she had so often seen him, in gym shorts, bare-chested with a sheen of sweat...

Side Edges

It was a dark night with only an occasional flash of light when the moon slid out from the clouds. The killer stomped along, anger seeping from pores. Stupid, stupid woman. Why couldn't she have kept her beaky nose out? It was all going fine. My plan was foolproof. Not one person suspected I killed the Colonel. Then she had to stick her beak in, causing me trouble. She deserves everything that's coming to her . She's making me do it. It's all her fault. Stay calm. I must stay calm.

Recovering A Slipped Stitch

The next morning the guests gradually drifted into the dining room until everyone was there except Josie and Mary. The Table was laid with cutlery, china and glasses of juice. Jazz came in carrying pots of tea and coffee placing them at intervals along the table. She took out her pad and pencil to take their orders for breakfast. Amid the general chatter and excitement about this morning's excursion to a woollen mill the guests helped themselves to cereal and fruit from the sideboard and tucked in.

Mary entered the dining room and scanned the guests looking for her sister. She moved closer to the table so the others could see her. "I'm sorry to interrupt but have any of you seen Josie this morning?"

Nobody had and Mary's face expressed her worry. "She wasn't in her bed when I woke up this morning, so I thought she might have come down early for breakfast."

"Perhaps she's gone for a walk in the gardens," Lucy suggested.

"Do you think she might have checked out after your row last night," May asked.

"I hadn't thought of that. It is the sort of thing she might do thinking she would make me feel guilty. I will go and ask Ursula."

"Do you want me to go with you?" May asked.

"No, stay and eat your breakfast."

Before she could leave, Jazz arrived with Mays and Lucy's breakfast.

"Have you seen my sister Josie this morning Jazz, I can't find her anywhere."

Jazz placed the plates in front of them. "No, I haven't."

May was concerned for Mary in her agitated state.

"I expect I'm panicking for no reason. Don't mind me carry on with your breakfast everyone." Mary said then left to find Ursula.

"You might be right, May. Perhaps she did change her mind about leaving. That was a hell of a ding-dong she had with her sister last night." Tony said.

"Yes but would she leave without telling her sister?" May asked.

May felt somewhat guilty, hoping her and Evelyns and Alices' cross words hadn't driven Josie away, they carried on eating their breakfasts in an uneasy silence.

Mary came back into the dining room, her face as white as the milk in the glass jug on the table. "Josie hasn't checked out, now I'm really worried." She said on the verge of tears.

"Come and sit down and have a cup of tea, it will help." May said.

Lucy poured May some tea and added milk.

"Have some breakfast and then we'll all go and look for her. It's too early to panic. She could have got a taxi home and not bothered to check out. Or gone for a walk in the gardens, try not to worry." May said.

"I don't think I can eat a thing. I know she hasn't left because

I've just been back up to our room and all her things are still there. I didn't stop to check when I came looking for her. She wouldn't go home without her things, even her handbag is there. I shouldn't have said all those nasty things to her last night, she must be really upset. I hope she hasn't done anything silly." Mary said, breaking down at last and sobbing into a napkin.

"Come on, this is Josie we're talking about, I obviously don't know her as well as you but I can't see her harming herself, she's too selfish." May said.

"May! Bit harsh" Michael whispered, "Mary's upset."

May whispered back, "I was only telling the truth."

Michael gave her a disapproving look.

"Have a little something to eat, there's no point in you feinting away. Look here is Jazz with some fresh toast, have a piece with some of this home-made marmalade, the sugar will make you feel better," Lucy said, always the carer, trying to encourage Mary. By the time everyone had finished their breakfasts Mary had managed only a tiny nibble of her toast to worried about her sister to eat.

Evelyn and Alice stood up from the table. "We are going up to our room to get ready for the outing. We're really excited about visiting the woollen mill. Sorry Mary, we really like you but your sister did the dirty on us. I'm sure she's hiding out just to pay you back for the things you said last night." The two women left quietly.

"Come on, troops, let's make this search quick because I'm looking forward to the mill tour too. Mary I think it would be better if you stayed here, in case Josie returns. Shall we split up, Me and Lucy will take all the fairy grottos and that area of the garden. Tony, would you and Michael head towards the veg gardens and nursery? And Sheila and Hazel can you take the front bit of the garden down towards the river. Shall we meet back here in fifteen minutes? That should still give us time to get ready for our outing." May said.

They all headed off to their apportioned bits of the gardens leaving the lonely figure of Mary sitting at the breakfast table.

Cast On Using Four Needles

"Do you think we should have told Ursula about Josie being missing?" Lucy asked as they headed through the sitting room towards the open French windows.

"I think she knows Lucy. Mary went to check if Josie had checked out, didn't she?"

"Oh yes, I didn't think of that."

May would have enjoyed the walk through the gardens if she hadn't started to feel anxious herself. The flowers were a picture especially the roses and the smell of Lavender was delicious as they brushed past the dainty purple heads overhanging the path. May had no idea why but she had an uneasy feeling about this search. Her nerve endings were tingling and she had to steel herself each time to enter the fairy grottoes but they didn't find Josie. They had searched them all and only had the shell house left. May had left it till last and she felt very apprehensive; she hadn't liked it the first time she had visited it. She had only gone in there on Ursula's insistence when they were enjoying the garden tour. She had found it quite claustrophobic and unpleasant unlike the fairy grottoes.

"Would you mind going in on your own May? I don't like it in there." Lucy said as she stood hesitatingly on the path.

"I'm not very keen either, I didn't like it the other day. Don't worry, I'll go you wait here." May said braver than she felt. Her hand shook as she switched on her phone torch and braced herself to enter the tunnel. At only five foot three inches she didn't need to but instinctively ducked through the rounded arched entry. You couldn't see into the grotto itself until you'd rounded the end of the tunnel which was low and narrow and completely covered with shells, even the roof; there wasn't a bare patch of wall to be seen.

This tunnel wasn't built for 21st century size 16 women like me, she thought. I can't even turn around, I'll either have to go forwards or shuffle backwards. I've got a really bad feeling about this place. I can feel the hairs on the back of my neck and arms standing on end. What if I'm right and the Colonel was murdered? What if Josie saw the killer? What if she's dead in there and the killer is still here? God, I feel sick. I wish I hadn't eaten that cooked breakfast, my stomach is swirling it around like the spin cycle on my washing machine. My feet won't move any further. What's that noise? Oh it's me breathing. Come on May don't be so feeble, deep breaths, in, out, in, out. It's only a cave with a bunch of old shells. With all these thoughts swirling around in her head May took another deep slow breath and started shuffling further into the tunnel. As well as the damp underground smell May now detected a faint metallic odour but nothing prepared her for the horror she was confronted with when she arrived inside the grotto.

"Are you okay in there May?" May could hear Lucy call from outside but was too shocked to answer. She was leaning on the wall at the end of the tunnel to the opening of the shell grotto. The metallic smell was stronger here. From the body a trail of blood went across the floor towards a spray of blood colouring the shells on the wall. Her legs were threatening to let her down. Her hand trembled as it held her phone which highlighted the grisly scene in front of her. Her other hand clung on tight to the edge of the wall, the shells cutting into her flesh not that she felt it. A scream was struggling to fight its way out but her throat was so tight it came out as a squeak. She didn't want to look but she couldn't stop, she couldn't move. Bile was bubbling up in her throat. She heard a sound from way behind her.

"May? I'm getting worried, I'm coming in," Lucy called from further back at the entrance to the tunnel.

The thought of Lucy seeing what she could see broke the nightmare spell May was trapped in. She swallowed and finally found her voice, even if it was a little shaky. She couldn't let Lucy see the horror that was in the grotto. "No! Stay there Lucy, I'm alright, I'm coming out."

Somehow May got her legs moving but she knew she couldn't enter into the grotto to turn around, shuffling backwards she made slow progress. As she groped the walls feeling her way, she dropped her phone plunging her in darkness. Panic almost overtook her but she managed to calm herself taking some deep breaths before she could carry on. She persevered shuffling back until she was at the entrance. Once outside her legs gave way and she sank down on the path. Scooching over until she could lean against the grotto wall she dropped her head between her knees as the nausea took over.

"Oh my God May, whatever has happened? What's wrong? You look as white as a sheet, er, well now you're turning green. Are you hurt?" Lucy crouched down beside her putting an arm around her back, she could feel May's body trembling.

"Lucy, go get help, it's Josie." May said without looking up.

"Is she hurt, shall I go in and help? I'm first aid trained."

"No! You need to go and get help."

"I'm not leaving you."

"You must, Please. I'll be fine, quick as you can."

Lucy stood up and put two fingers to her lips and let out three sharp blasts, one of the loudest whistles May had ever heard.

"Help! Tony! Michael! Sheila! Hazel! Over here at the shell grotto! help!" She shouted then did another three piercing whistles.

"Wow, when did you learn to do that, in the boy scouts?" May asked her words muffled as she still had her head down between her knees, hoping to forestall any questions Lucy was bound to ask.

Lucy wasn't fooled, she knew something awful had happened but realised that May wasn't yet able to say what she'd seen and was making small talk for the sake of it. "Believe it or not, a seven year old girl on a library trip that was getting out of hand. I couldn't make the little rascals hear me over their noise and she let out this piercing whistle from her little body that stopped them in their tracks.That was definitely something I needed to learn. "

"Well it's a very useful skill, you will have to teach me." May sat up and rested her head back on the entrance wall, not sure she could stand yet.

Tony and Michael arrived panting as they ran down the path. followed a few minutes later by Sheila and Walters.

"Hazel has gone back to the house to stay with Mary, we thought it was better she didn't come until we knew what we were dealing with." Sheila said.

"Good thinking." May said.

"What is going on May, are you hurt?" Walters asked.

May got to her feet, helped by Tony and Walters. "You need to call the police urgently nine, nine, nine. Josie is in the grotto," she paused, "she's dead."

"Oh my God no. Poor Mary. I've got my phone I'll do it," Sheila turned back towards the house and walked a short distance, pulling her phone out and dialling.

"Are you sure she's dead? I'd better go in and check." Walters made a move towards the entrance.

"No!" May shouted. "Mr Walters. Please believe me, she is dead and it is definitely not natural causes. We mustn't disturb anything until the police get here." As the image of Josie filled her head once more tears started trickling down her cheeks.

"You're in shock, come on, let's get you back to the house," Lucy moved back to May and gave her a side hug, slipping her arm through and pulling her in tight.

May turned to Tony. "Tony, will you stay here with Mr Walters until the police arrive?"

Walters frowned at May. "You can trust me not to go in you know."

"It's for your protection as well Mr Walters. Now you can both confirm that neither of you have been inside except me." May sagged a little.

"Lucy, Michael, get her back to the house, she's in shock. May, we'll guard the shell house until the police arrive, don't worry. You can trust us. We'll make sure nobody goes in, won't we mate?" Tony affirmed.

Walters nodded, still looking disgruntled and turned his back on May.

As they neared the terrace of the house May stopped. "I can't face Mary yet. I can't tell her what I saw, I just can't," she started sobbing.

"Ssh, it's okay. We can go in the back door to the kitchen and I'll make you a nice hot cup of tea with a brandy on the side for the shock." Michael led them across the terrace, past the kitchen herb garden, opening the door and ushering them through..

"I'll put the kettle on," Lucy said

Michael sat May down on one of the Kitchen chairs and placed both hands on her shoulders and looked into her eyes. "I know it's hard May but try not to think about what you've seen. I'm going to fetch you a brandy."

"I don't think I shall ever forget what I've seen." May's tears fell again and Lucy reached for some kitchen roll, pulling off a wad and passing it to May. Michael patted May on the shoulder and left to fetch a brandy from the bar.

There was no sign of Nancy or Jazz but as the schedule was for the guests to go out for the morning as well as having lunch out, that was not surprising. May was glad of the quiet and Lucy's gentle presence, she tried not to think about Josie.

Charts For Moss Stitch & Ribbing

DI Carley, DS Flower and DS Perrot were huddled together on the path leading to the shell grotto waiting for the scene of crime officers to finish their investigations. Tony and Walters had been sent back into the house with instructions to tell everyone to stay in the house and wait to be interviewed.

"This is a whole different ball game and puts a different complexion on the Colonel's death. Damn it we only released his body yesterday. Sonya, can you find Mrs Jeffries and find out which undertaker has the Colonel. Get in touch with them straight away and arrange for the body to be taken back to the morgue. Let's hope she didn't ask for him to be embalmed."

"Sir." Sonya said then turned on the path and made her way back to the house.

"Hey Ho chaps." Simon Green the Forensic Pathologist came puffing down the path, tipping his fedora at Sonya as they passed each other. "Lovely morning for it. 'Come into the garden Maud' and I'll pop you off amongst the daisies." he trilled, beaming. "Where's the cadaver?"

"Do you have to be so damn cheerful Simon? She's in the shell grotto."

"It's the only way in my job, Carley, dealing with the horrors of humanity every day. Bit of luck, those SOCO lot being here, nothing like on the job training." He suited up in the protective gear, pulled plastic shoe covers on and a pair of blue latex gloves. Then he attempted to enter the grotto but his shoulders were too wide so he turned sideways as he thought that would make it easier and waved jovially at DI Carley & DS Perrot unfortunately he then got stuck in the entrance.

"He's just like Winnie the Pooh stuck in rabbit's hole," chuckled DS Perrot

"Still reading kids books Davey?" DICarley grinned, also amused at the rotund pathologist gamely trying to squeeze his way in.

The pathologist's height wasn't the problem but his girth was, he was never going to be able to enter sideways. He wriggled his way back out then rolled his substantial shoulders inwards, arms out in front, hands together clutching his bag and forced his way in calling back as he went. "I shall hear you if you start laughing."

DI Carley and DS Perrott grinned at each other. It was these moments that made their often distressing job easier. This was definitely a story to share back at the station. Luckily in this part of the world, murders were few and far between. North Devon was a low crime area even though it had its share of low grade villains.

After about twenty minutes the two SOCO's stooping came out of the entrance and beckoned the two detectives over. They were already dressed in their protective gear and ready to go. "There's not much room in there sir, We'll wait out here. The doc's ready for you."

Carley had a similar problem to the pathologist, although not as round he had a stocky build with broad shoulders that stuck in the entrance. He had to manoeuvre sideways to be able to enter. "Not a word, Perrott, not a word."

DS Perrott pressed his lips together holding in his mirth as his boss squeezed into the entrance but soon had a similar problem himself. Crouching because his six foot frame didn't fit into the

Victorian sized tunnel any easier than his colleagues. "If it's any consolation sir, I'm struggling too. It's my height as well as my muscular arms." he grimaced as he forced himself through the narrow space, knowing his suit jacket was being assaulted by the shells on the walls.

"Muscular arms? Stop showing off Perrott, I'm not your girlfriend. Muscular arms, he muttered"

Somehow the three men managed to squeeze into the small grotto, keeping close to the tunnel side and careful to tread on the protective squares laid out by the SOCOs'. The body lay feet towards the entrance, head to the back wall and was lit by bright white lamps on sturdy tripods. Trying not to knock the lights over they leaned forward so they could get a closer look at the body.

What he saw made DS Perrott glad he had missed breakfast.

"She was skewered to death. I've never seen anything like it before. I won't remove them until I get her back to the lab but I think these are double ended steel knitting needles. See the way they have entered? It looks like the way my granny used to knit socks. They are crossed over each other to form a circle in the centre where the sock would be but in this case her neck. But look here." The forensic pathologist pointed to a needle on the right hand side of her neck. "Someone knew their anatomy. The first needle probably killed her, it's straight into the jugular vein. That's where that spray of blood came from." He pointed to the ground and the splatter on the wall. "The second needle has pierced the interior jugular on the left hand side. The third has pierced the Anterior jugular and the last one, I'm guessing at this point, straight through the trachea. I'll be able to confirm it when I get her onto the slab. She also has a contusion on the right hand side of her head and on the back."

"What caused the head wounds, anything found in here?" Carley asked.

"Bit early to say for sure but something hard, smooth and

round about the size of my palm. Something like the round smooth stones at Westward Ho! It wasn't big but then it didn't need to be, it caught her smack bang on the temple. As I say someone knew what they were doing."

"What do you think happened here doc?" Carley asked.

"From the position of the body it looks like she was facing the entrance when her killer entered. There are no signs of a struggle, no obvious residue in her fingernails so she was probably expecting whoever it was." The pathologist mimed the actions as he spoke. "The killer entered with the round stone concealed in his or her hand. They were right handed by the way. They swung and hit her on the side of the temple, causing her to fall backwards hitting her head on the concrete floor causing the wound to the back of the head. Then I think whilst she was dazed or unconscious the killer then skewered her."

"God, so she was still alive. A man or a woman do you think?"

"Either. The victim isn't very tall, five feet three inches or thereabouts and those needles are sharp and strong. If a woman was angry enough it's definitely possible, it wouldn't take enormous strength to push them in. It was pretty brutal."

"Two deaths in the same place in the same week are a coincidence too far for me Simon. I've already requested the Colonel's body be returned to the morgue. I'm sorry to ask this but do you think you could have missed something?" DI Carley asked.

Before the pathologist could answer DS Parrott interrupted. "Sir, I've been looking over the statements from the witnesses to the Colonel's death and I think I missed something."

"Well don't keep it to yourself laddie, share the glad tidings." The pathologist said, a tinge of annoyance in his voice at being interrupted.

"The SOCOs' didn't find any glasses or decanters at the scene of the Colonel's death."

"No there definitely weren't any or I would have seen them too." DI Carley interrupted.

"They weren't there when I examined the body." Simon confirmed.

"In May's statement," DS Perrott carried on

"Who's May?" DI Carley interrupted.

"One of the guests. She was the first on the scene after Nancy the cook discovered the Colonel's body." He glanced at his tablet, "Ms Wood said there was definitely an empty glass resting between the Colonel's groin and thigh and a decanter on the table." He looked up. "Someone must have removed them both before we arrived and cordoned the terrace off."

"Good work Davey but how the hell did you miss that in the first place? We'll talk about that later back at the station. I hope you haven't made any plans as you'll be doing a lot of late shifts. Let's get back to the house and start the interviews." DI Carley said.

"Before you go, do we know who she is?" The forensic pathologist asked, nodding his head at the body.

"Yes, I remember her. Josie Mathers, she's here with her sister. A very difficult woman, looks like she upset the wrong person. Doc, can you concentrate on the Colonel first? There must be something we've all missed. I'm surmising if the decanter and glass were removed we may be looking at poison." DI Carley said.

"I didn't find anything with the standard toxicology tests but I do have some other more specialist tests up my sleeve. I'm going to enjoy this. I don't like to be proved wrong." The forensic pathologist said, rubbing his hands together with glee.

DI Carley moved towards the tunnel. "Thanks doc. I know you don't need me to ask but as soon as you get something, let me know asap."

"Will do, will do." The pathologist answered, gazing down at the body already lost in thought.

The two detectives walked along the path towards the house, meeting DS Flower on the way. They stopped on the terrace.

"DS Flower, did you talk to Mrs Jeffries?"

"Yes sir, I told her that she cannot go ahead with the funeral and that we will be carrying out further tests on her husband?"

"How did she take it?"

"Surprised at first, then she looked scared to me, didn't shed a tear though."

"Mmm. Okay, can you start interviewing the other guests in the dining room."

"Sir." DS Flower affirmed.

DS Perrott, go and talk to Ms Wood again? See what she can remember about the decanter and glass. Do you think she's a competent witness?"

"Yes sir. Actually I know Ms Wood, her best friend is my lodger. She's a great girl, very observant, she has to be in her job."

"Oooh!" DS Flower smirked at him.

"Why didn't you say you knew her?" DI Carley narrowed his eyes and looked at him keenly. "Anything going on between you two?"

DS Flower made herself scarce, she'd rib DS Perrott about it later though.

Davey felt himself go hot as he remembered the last time he had seen May in his flat. She'd been having a sleepover with Trudy and was fresh from a shower. It was the first time he had properly really noticed her. Up till then she'd just been Trudy's friend with the crappy boyfriend. With her face bare of make-up and ringlets of damp hair she was even more beautiful. Wearing a pair of shorts-style pyjamas with cartoon pigs all over them she was stretched out on one end of the sofa, a glass of wine in her hand. Trudy his flat mate was at the opposite end and the women's feet were tangled together. He was sitting in his usual armchair, they had all been watching a James Bond movie and they had kept him laughing with their smutty comments about Daniel Craig. Only getting worse when he jokingly told them off for their inappropriate comments. He flushed red when he realised his superior was talking to him and he hadn't heard a single word.

"Sorry sir, didn't quite catch that."

"Perrott! Snap out of it. You need to focus, this is a murder investigation. I asked you if there was anything going on between you and the witness and by the look on your soppy face it looks like a possibility." DI Carley didn't hide his irritation. With possibly two murders on his hands he needed his team to be on it, not mooning after one of the witnesses. He'd have his super breathing down his neck any minute, because he'd have the chief constable breathing down his.

"Sorry sir. No sir, nothing between us. She's just a friend of my flatmate. I only see her occasionally but I do know her well enough to know she is honest and has an advanced DBS check for her job. She will make a good witness."

"Good, let's keep it professional, we don't need anything to jeopardise this investigation. Actually now I think about it, it might actually help that you know her. She should feel comfortable with you and you might get a lot more out of her. Ask her when exactly she saw the glass and decanter and if she can remember the time they went missing. It could be crucial. Also anything she can tell us about Josie Mathers. She's been with the woman all week, she must know something. I'm going to interview the deceased's sister Mary Winter. We'll meet back in Mrs Jeffries office. If you get there before me, start plotting everyone's movements from when they were last altogether, probably at dinner last night. Don't let them leave a thing out, the tiniest detail could help us. Get going."

"Sir." He followed DI Carley along the path, he wasn't sure his boss was right that May would feel comfortable with him. That night of the James Bond movie, he hadn't been able to sleep and he'd gone to the kitchen to get himself a glass of milk. He hadn't put any lights on or made a noise as May was sleeping on the couch. He'd been tempted to look at her sleeping but thought it was too creepy, so he'd carried on to the kitchen, bumping into her in the darkness of the doorway. She would have gone flying if he hadn't caught hold of her around her waist. She didn't struggle, in fact she moved closer to him, she felt so good. Then he remembered she had only recently split up with her boyfriend. He dropped a kiss on the top of her head and stepped away. Neither of them said anything and he hadn't seen her since that night but there was definitely chemistry between them. When he had interviewed her there was definitely a moment between them a spark of attraction . He knew he shouldn't have touched her when he guided her out of the dining room but he hadn't been able to help himself.

Godets in Knitting

Davey stopped at the kitchen door, took a deep breath and prepared to be friendly but professional. All his plans flew out the window when he saw May, her eyes were red from weeping and she had a bunch of soggy tissue screwed up in her hand. She looked so small and helpless, he started towards her then that creep Ryder dropped into the chair next to her, putting his arm around her and pulling her into his side looking at Davey with a smirk on his face. Davey involuntarily clenched his fists. What he wouldn't give to wipe that smug look off the man's face but he stayed calm knowing that in fact he had the upper hand in this situation. He moved close to May and hunched down next to her chair speaking to her softly.

"Hi there May, how are you doing? I can see you're upset, that's only natural you've had a terrible shock but I need to ask you some questions, it's really important if we are to catch Josie's killer."

"She's not in any state to answer questions, you'll have to wait till later." Ryder said.

"Time is of the essence if we are to catch Josie's killer," Davey shot back.

The two men glared at each other but May wasn't about to

get stuck in the middle of whatever was going on between them. She pulled away from Ryder and sat up straight, turning towards him. "I don't need anyone to speak for me thank you, I'm quite capable." She looked up at Davey who was now standing in front of her. "Where do you want me?"

Their eyes locked and Davey suddenly felt too hot in his suit jacket.

Ryder stood up abruptly, invading Davey's space, the two glared at each other.

"Oh for goodness sake." May stood up and grabbed Davey's hand. "Come on let's go into the garden, I need some fresh air anyway. Thank you for looking after me Ryder. Will you be okay Lucy?"

Lucy had been sitting on the other side of May, she stood up too. "I'll be fine. I'll clear up here then I'll go up to my room until they want to talk to me." She left the kitchen through the door to the hallway.

Davey was startled when May took his hand but enjoyed the sensation of her hand in his. He smiled smugly back at Ryder as May pulled him along and walked them both to the back door of the Kitchen and out into the garden. They both stopped when they found a quiet spot with a bench secluded by hedges and they both sat down.

"Are you sure you are okay to talk to me May?" He was still holding her hand.

She didn't pull her hand away, "Yes, I didn't like Josie but she didn't deserve to die."

In The Garden

"Before we talk about that can I take you back to the day of the Colonel's death?" He let go of her hand to pull out his tablet and tapped the screen.

"The Colonel? I thought you wanted to know about Josie? I thought you had decided the Colonel's death was a natural death."

"In light of Josie's murder we have to look at the Colonel's death again. In your statement to me you said that when you arrived on the terrace Nancy was next to the Colonel and there was a glass resting on his body and a decanter on the table. Can you go through that again for me please? From when you first arrived on the terrace."

"I rushed downstairs and straight to the sitting room and tried to get out through the French doors but they were locked and it took me a few seconds to unlock them. Nancy was on the Colonel's left side leaning over her hand on his shoulder. A whisky glass was resting in the crease between his groin and his thigh, it was empty. The decanter was on the table next to him."

"You're doing really well May. Was there anything in the decanter?"

May closed her eyes and thought back to the scene on the patio. "Yes I'm sure there was still some whisky in the decanter about a third of the way up from the bottom."

"How do you know it was whisky?"

"Well I suppose I assumed it was because that's what the Colonel had been drinking every night but there was also the decanter." May said.

"What about the decanter?"

"It was cut glass and had a silver Whisky label hung around the neck by a chain."

"Well done May, that's really useful information. Your powers of observation are excellent. Now this is the tricky bit, when did you notice they had disappeared?" Davey asked. He was trying hard to concentrate and stay professional but it was hard with Mays bare thigh pressing against him.

May closed her eyes again, somehow it helped her to recall those scenes out of her memory. "I'm not exactly sure but everyone had left the terrace except for me and Ursula, Mrs

Jeffries. I had stopped to talk to her. Yes, I remember now, I was looking back at the Colonel across the terrace and I noticed the decanter was gone but I'm absolutely positive the glass was still there. It must have been one of the others who took the decanter when we were all distracted watching Nancy and Ursula rowing"

"Okay, good. Now do you remember when the glass went missing?"

"No, I'm sorry, because I didn't go back to the terrace till the afternoon's workshop. Davey?" She leant towards him laying her hand on his thigh, instantly she could feel his muscles contract, her eyes flew to his face and she took her hand away. "Look I've made a few notes, I don't know if they will help." Embarrassed, she searched the pocket of her denim shorts then handed the list over to Davey.

Davey moved away slightly allowing a little space between them. He didn't trust himself, he was trying to remain professional but his body was acting like a lovestruck teenager. He took the note and cleared his throat, looking out at the garden not trusting himself to look at her.

"May, did anything happen with Josie yesterday that might have made someone angry enough to harm her?"

May thought back to Mary's argument with her sister and Evelyn and Hazels then flushed as she remembered her own argument with Josie after dinner. "Well, she was nasty to everyone really, I think we all had words with her over the past week."

"Anybody in particular? What was her sister Mary's relationship with her like?"

May wasn't about to tell him the problems between the sisters, no way was she going to put the idea of Mary being a suspect in his mind. "Josie was difficult but Mary had the patience of a saint and seemed to know how to handle her. They must have got on okay because they were on this holiday together."

He turned to look at her, sure she was hiding something. "Anybody else come to mind?"

"No." May couldn't look at him because she knew she wasn't

a very good liar." I can't think of anybody or anything else. Can I go now?"

"Yes, but if you think of anything, however small or unimportant you think it is, ring me." He pressed a business card into her hand, folded her fingers over the top and covered it with his own. His voice softened. "You've had an awful shock May, I must admit I've never seen anything like it before it shocked us all. You need to take care of yourself. We'll arrange for Victim Support to contact you but would you like me to arrange for you to go home?"

"No, but thank you, I want to see the week out. Apart from a couple of murders I'm enjoying myself." She looked down at his hand over hers and smiled at him.

"I'll look at your notes but promise me no sleuthing on your own, it's dangerous. This isn't a film or a book, this is real. Be careful and stay with the others, there's a possibility someone here has killed twice now." He said.

"Stay with the others? It's one of them that's got to be the murderer!" She gave a nervous chuckle.

"You know what I mean. Look out for yourself. I care about you and don't want you to be hurt." He looked up as DS Flower appeared and cleared her throat to attract his attention.

She wondered what she'd interrupted. Davey looked earnest and May well she wasn't sure what that look on her face was but they had definitely been holding hands.

"Sorry to interrupt. Can I have a quick word, Davey?" Sonya asked.

"Yes, we've finished here anyway." He rose and with a smile at May walked over to his colleague.

May stood up too but Sonya stopped her from leaving.

"Can you stay there a minute for me ma'am?" Taking Davey's arm she pulled him out of earshot.

"Did she tell you about the arguments after dinner last night?"

Davey looked at May quickly then back to Sonya. "No, she only said that they had all had words at some time with the deceased.

"I've been interviewing two of the women," she glanced at her tablet, "Evelyn and Alice, they positively enjoyed telling me everything. Mary had a huge row with her sister last night and all sorts of info came out. Apparently they have been in conflict for a long time about an inheritance from their parents. It all came to a head last night when Josie told Mary she was going to change her will and Mary wouldn't now inherit. Evelyn and Alice both admitted to threatening her about a knitting pattern but they didn't threaten to murder her. Then May had an argument with Josie and told her she would die alone. I've updated Carley and he's tackling Mary again. I'm going to carry on interviewing the other guests. You need to get her talking Davey, she knows more than she's saying. See you back in Ursula's office."

"Thanks Sonya." He looked at May still sitting on the bench. Why didn't she mention the rows after dinner? He knew she'd been holding something back but because of her distressed state he thought it could wait till later but he had no choice now, he couldn't let his attraction cloud his judgement. In his heart he truly didn't believe she was a killer but in his job he knew that sometimes people can act completely out of character when pushed. Not looking forward to it he went and sat back down, this time making sure he had plenty of space between them.

"May I want to go back to last night again. Can you talk me through what happened after dinner again and this time don't leave anything out." He had to give her another chance to tell him the truth.

May wasn't stupid, she realised that one of the others must have blabbed about the rows last night to the other detective. She felt extremely uncomfortable about not telling Davey and realised the police could find this suspicious. She apologised for not telling him the truth before, although as she pointed out it was more an omission. Then she went through her story again but this time telling him about the arguments between Josie, Mary, Evelyn and Alice and herself.

"Why didn't you tell me this before May. What are you trying to hide?"

"I wasn't trying to hide anything. I didn't want to get Mary into trouble."

"Are you sure you weren't just protecting yourself? Davey felt bad about pushing her but he had to do his job.

"No! Of course not. I didn't kill her."

"Yet you found the body. Did you go back to the scene in case you had left DNA there when you killed her?"

May shot up off the bench. "What is this Davey? Am I a suspect now just because I had a bit too much wine and gave Josie a few home truths?" If that's the case then all of the guests should be suspects. And what about his wife? Or her lover? I can't believe you would even think this of me. I don't think I'm going to answer any more of your questions." It was all too much for May, seeing Josie's horrific death this morning and now Davey who she was falling for and thought he felt the same accusing her of murder.

He saw her tears before she'd had the chance to turn away and walk back into the house. He felt rotten, he hated that he'd made her cry but the fact was she was a suspect. With leaden feet he followed May slowly back to the house and headed for the office.

Cable Stitch Patterns

By the time DI Carley and DS Flower turned up in Ursula's office, Davey had produced a timeline of events. He'd written it out in large print with a black felt tip he'd found in the desk drawer on printing paper from the photocopier and stuck them on the walls.

"Ah, good lad, that's going to help because at the moment I'm struggling to make sense of what's gone on here." He walked up to the wall. "I've let them all go off on their excursion, none of them look like they are going to run away. They would have done so before the body was found if that was the case. The cook and the waitress will be in later and I've tasked PC Styles to stay and take their separate statements when they arrive. He sat down in Ursula's office chair and looked at Sonya, who was one of his most experienced detectives. She was good at evaluating people's non-verbal cues and he valued her insight. Often she would spot something the others had missed .

"What do you reckon's been going on here then Sonya?"

She sat herself down in one of the office chairs next to Davey, she had been studying the timeline on the wall.

"As I see it there could be two possible scenarios."

"Go on," Carley said.

"The first death the Colonels' could have been the result of the eternal triangle. The deceased's wife is having an affair with her butler, sounds like Downton Abbey doesn't it?" she giggled grinning at Davey.

"Yes, very funny, get on with it." Carley said, his lips twitching trying not to smile.

"Sorry sir. I think we should look into the finances of this place and Ursula and the Colonels personal finance'. This was a private home until very recently and the pair were very much of the horse and hound set. I'm guessing they may be short of money which is why they've turned the place into a hotel. Then there's Ursula and Walters' affair. Did she kill the Colonel so that she could marry Walters? Or did she kill him because he has used all her money and was now drinking away any profits they might make? If it turns out he was poisoned, that is often a female method." She glanced down at her tablet. "According to the Colonel's nephew, Ryder, he sounds like he should be in a Jilly Cooper book." She grinned at Davey who looked bemused.

Carley cleared his throat.

Sonya hastily picked up where she left off. "Ryder says his uncle drank like a fish and he always thought he would kill himself with booze and cigars one day. But the other thing he said which his wife hasn't mentioned is that he's an inveterate gambler and he has gambled most of his wife's fortune away and he thinks he might have some outstanding debts. He also said that Ursula has lost most of her social circle of friends because the Colonel involved them in dodgy money making schemes where they lost thousands. She definitely has a motive for killing him. Walters could have done it to secure his position with Ursula, if he marries her he gets all this. What I can't see is why either of them would kill Josie, a guest they had never met before she arrived this week. There doesn't seem to be a connection between the two deaths and we still don't know for sure that the Colonel was murdered. It's more than likely that Josie's sister Mary finally snapped and killed her before she could change her will which she had threatened to do last night."

"Well done Sonya, I can always rely on you to make sense of things. What about you Davey? What do you think?."

Davey sat up straighter in his chair. "I believe the two deaths are connected. I absolutely agree with Sonya that either Ursula or Walters could have done it, they were both hiding something in their interviews, equally there's a possibility that Ryder did it. We haven't looked into whether the Colonel had a will and who inherits after his death. Let's assume for the moment that the Colonel was murdered. Isn't it a possibility that Josie could have either seen who did it, after all her bedroom window overlooks the terrace or seen who removed the glass and decanter. She was a nasty bit of work by all accounts. She had already possibly committed fraud with her aunt's will and pocketed the money and was now refusing to hand over her sister's share of their parents inheritance. Money was obviously important to her. What if she tried to blackmail the murderer and got herself killed to silence her?"

"It's a bit of a leap to go from a nasty woman who wouldn't share an inheritance to being a blackmailer Davey."

"I'm not so sure Sonya, Davey has pointed out a workable theory. Right whilst we're waiting on the lab reports, plan of action. Sonya, can you look into the financial background of Ursula Jeffries and the nephew Ryder, find out how he earns his money, that Porsche cost a bob or two."

Sonya smiled at her boss's antiquated sayings, what the hell was a bob? "Yes sir."

"I'm going to concentrate on Walters, he's a bit of a mystery man. Davey, you look into the Colonel, I want to know where he gambles, any debts, all about the money making schemes and a list of people who lost money on them. You never know we might find someone with a bigger motive than our suspects. Talking of which Ursula Jeffries, Walters, Mary Beale and May Wood are our prime suspects for the moment. Let's get back to the station and get cracking." Carley rose from the office chair. "You'd better pull all that off the wall and bring it with us Davey. Let's hope the Doc comes up with something soon."

Davey stood and collected the timeline papers off the wall and followed his colleagues out. He couldn't help but worry about May being a suspect.

Casting Off

Once the police had gone and the guests were off albeit late to their excursion, Walters made coffee for himself and Ursula. They sat on the terrace on the opposite side from where the Colonel had died.

"Are you okay?" Walters asked, reaching across the table and taking her hand in his.

"Oh yes I'm absolutely fine. It's the very first week of opening our hotel, my husband dies and a guest gets murdered." Ursula replied, pulling her hand away and sipping her coffee.

"Don't be like that, you know what I mean. Surely it's a relief the old bastard dying like that. You don't have to go through all the rigmarole of divorcing him now. This woman dying is an inconvenience and a weird coincidence but it's nothing to do with us." He tried to take her hand again.

Ursula didn't say anything for a moment as she gazed down the slope of the garden to the river below. He waited, he knew he couldn't push her, she'd talk when she was ready. After a few minutes she turned to him.

"Are you aware, the police have taken his body back from the undertakers for more tests?"

Shocked, his face paled. "When did this happen and why

didn't you tell me?" He stood up and paced up and down in front of their table before finally dropping back in his seat again. "What made them decide to do more tests?"

Ursula looked at him, he was good looking and very useful but he really wasn't the sharpest knife in the drawer. If she had met him before she had met the Colonel there is no way they would ever have become lovers. And now with the Colonel dead and she was free to marry him she knew that she wouldn't. He was attractive and a good lover but he would never be equal to her social standing. Now she was free she wanted to gain some of the life she had before she met the Colonel. It would be hard but she still had the odd friend in the right places. She would start her by dipping her toe in the social calendar at the golf club. She was brought out of her reverie by Walters.

"Ursula, I asked you why do they want his body back? I thought they had agreed it was a heart attack and signed the death certificate?"

"The Inspector told me in light of a second death in the same place in less than a week they had to look again at the Colonel's death. I asked him how that woman had died but he wouldn't tell me?"

Walters got up and started pacing again. "Damn that woman. She was trouble from the moment she arrived. Let's hope that it is just procedure and there's nothing to find, she must have had a stroke or something. We'll be okay. We just need to stay calm" He moved behind her chair and placed his hands on her shoulders. Even though he felt her tense beneath his fingers he moved in and kissed the side of her neck, behind her ear her sensitive spot. "While we have the place to ourselves, let's go upstairs."

She stood abruptly and stepped away from him. "Don't be so stupid. We need to keep our relationship strictly professional until all this is over.

She had called him stupid once to often, he scowled at her and left the terrace slamming the French door behind him making the glass rattle.

The Auto Heel

May was relieved to get back to her sock knitting this afternoon on the terrace. The weather was still glorious and with the shelter of the sunshades and a slight breeze it should have been the perfect spot to relax, if she was able. Even the trip to the woollen mill would have been far more enjoyable if she still hadn't been worried about her interview this morning with Davey. She couldn't quite work out how she had managed to become a suspect, not that he had said anything but from his questioning she was certain that she was. It was crazy, she had no real motive, she had only met the woman a few days ago. She wasn't a psychopath and someone was seriously deranged to carry out that horrific murder. She made a conscious effort to relax, dropping her shoulders which were up around her ears and taking some deep breaths.

"Are you alright May?" Lucy asked with a worried frown on her face.

"Yes, just a bit out of whack with what's been going on. Even when you know you're not, when the police question you it makes you feel like a criminal." May replied shakily.

"I'm sorry May, it's my fault. I shouldn't have told that woman detective about the rows last night. She was like a dog with a bone once I let it slip and I'm terrible at lying. I felt compelled to tell her everything." Lucy said tearfully.

"It's fine Lucy, no one would want you to lie but it has made the police look at me and Mary with suspicion." May said.

Now she no longer had her sister to sit with Mary had joined their table and she arrived just in time to hear what May said. "I don't think the police are suspicious of us at all May, why would you think that? The nice policeman who talked to me this morning was very kind and a proper gentleman. He told me he quite understood why I hadn't wanted to say anything bad about my sister now she had passed. Then when he asked me about our aunt and our parents, I told him everything she had done and he agreed with me that she had been selfish keeping our inheritance to herself. Oh no dear, we don't have anything to worry about. Of course I'm very upset that Josie died. After all she was my sister and it came right out of the blue because she hadn't been ill at all. It must have been a stroke or something, sadly that can happen at our age." Mary dabbed at her tears.

Tony exchanged an incredulous look with May, "Naive or what." He said under his breath to May. "Like a lamb to the slaughter."

Whilst Mary was dipping into her tote for her knitting, May leaned over and whispered in Tony's ear. "Nobody knows yet but Josie was murdered."

Tony's jaw dropped, when he regained his power of speech he whispered back, "Tell me all afters."

Michael, always the one to smooth awkward moments over said, "Let's try and forget about everything for a few hours and concentrate on our knitting. We only have this afternoon and tomorrow morning's session then we'll be off home."

"Well said my love, no more talk of murder, let's knit. Thank you for helping me with my heel flap Lucy. I would never have ished in time for this afternoon's lesson." Tony looked up as ody answered him, he realised something was up but didn't what.

"Tony, you said the 'm' word," Michael whispered to him.

Luckily he was saved by Ivy who had called for their attention. He could have kicked himself, he knew he shouldn't have mentioned murder, now Mary would curious and might ask him what he meant. She looked at him then shook her head as if to clear it and looked towards Ivy, much to his relief.

Turning The Heel

"Good afternoon everyone. I'm not going to mention this morning's distressing event, I have already had a quiet word with Mary and she would like us to carry on. So have we all finished knitting our heel flap?"

Everyone assured her they had.

"Brilliant. In these boxes on the table there is an extra little present for you all. Stitch markers, you may choose two each as you will need them for the next bit." She waited for them to choose their markers and return to their chairs before continuing then held up the sock that she was using to demonstrate. "Now the magic happens, we are going to turn our heel. It's one of my favourite parts of knitting a sock because you knit a few rows and a heel appears as if by magic"

"I struggled with the heel flap Ivy, I've a feeling I am going to make a pig's ear out of turning the heel." Tony said gloomily.

"I promise you will all get the hang of it, just watch me then follow the instructions on the pattern ." Ivy slowly went through the process of turning the heel a row at a time, so that they could follow along and then went around checking that everyone had managed it. When everyone had turned their heels it was time to break for tea and cake as Jazz and Walters were already on their way across the terrace.

After tea they moved on to the gusset, which took up the rest of the afternoon. By the end everyone was well on their way and they all had a piece of knitting that was beginning to look like a sock.

"If you want to carry on knitting then that is probably a good idea because tomorrow once your sock is long enough I want to show you how to close the toe with Kitchener stitch. Then if we have any time over you can start your second sock. You have a free morning tomorrow, our last day and I look forward to seeing you all at two o'clock as usual. We won't stop for a tea break then as Ursula is providing a cream tea at the end of our last session before you leave for home."

There were lots of oohs and a chatter of excitement at the thought of another proper Devon cream tea.

"Thank you all for another enjoyable afternoon."

Tony started clapping and they all joined in with shouts of 'thanks Ivy'

Ivy packed her things up and left the terrace along with Sheila and Hazel who had started chatting to her about yarn. On the far side of the terrace, Evelyn and Alice were soon deep in conversation, their needles flying in and out of their socks. Mary had excused herself, saying she was going to her room as she had some more phone calls to make.

Frogging Back

Lucy was attempting to put Tony's sock right after he had started reversing his heel decreasings on his gusset and Michael was pouring them a cup of tea out of the fresh teapot they had ordered.

"Come on then spill the beans, what happened to Josie?"

May looked around but there was nobody within earshot. She was fiddling with a piece of sponge cake that she hadn't been able to eat and crumbled it with her fingers.

Lucy realised May was still upset. "You don't have to tell us May. Tony, if you'd been there when May first came out of that grotto, you would have realised that she'd seen something she might not want to talk about."

"Sorry May, I'm an insensitive twit at times, you ask Michael."

"It's true." Michael confirmed.

"Oy, you don't have to agree with me," Tony laughed, giving Michael a quick elbow jab to his ribs. Sorry May, I've got a bit carried away, you must admit it is like being in an Agatha Christy murder mystery especially as we are staying in an old house in Devon." Tony said.

May couldn't help but smile at Tony. She too was a lover of the Agatha Christie novels and was happy to watch old reruns of

Poirot or Miss Marple on the tv." You're right Tony it is like an Agatha Christie, let's hope it stays like that and doesn't turn into a 'Midsomer Murders' their villages are littered with murders every episode." May laughed and the others joined in.

May grew serious again. "I'm not supposed to tell anyone what I saw but I don't think any of you are the killer. It would really help me to talk it through. I need some friends on my side." She took a deep breath. When I went into the grotto I found Josie dead on the floor. There was a lot of blood, some had even sprayed up the wall." May paused, "She had four knitting needles sticking out of her neck."

There was a collective gasp from the listeners.

"Blimmen heck May! You predicted it, you said she'd be murdered with a knitting needle in the grotto..." His voice tailed off as he realised what he'd said.

They were all looking shocked and in a small voice May said. "I can't believe I said that. I was only joking. I wouldn't, I didn't mean." It was too much for her and she broke down sobbing her head on her arms on the table.

"Now look what you've done." Michael was cross. "May, we don't believe for a minute you would do anything like that. It was a joke, no more than that. It must be a weird coincidence. We all joined in on the joke. It could be any one of us and I'm sure we've all said something similar this week about Josie. It doesn't mean we meant it."

"We won't tell the police you said it, Michael is right it was just a joke." Tony said, patting her on the back.

"We know you couldn't hurt anyone May. We promise not to say anything. Here you are drink your tea, it will help." Lucy held her cup out to her, rubbing comforting circles on her back.

May wiped her tears on the bottom of her t-shirt and took the tea cup looking at them over the rim as she drank. Remembering that Lucy had told May earlier that she was a terrible liar and had already spilled the beans about the arguments; she just had to hope that her ill-advised comment didn't reach the police's ears.

. . .

That hope was dashed almost instantly as DS Perrott came through the French windows and onto the terrace followed by a female constable.

"Ms Wood, we would like you to accompany us to the police station in Barnstaple to answer a few more questions." Davey forced himself to stay neutral even though seeing the fear on May's face was like a dagger to his heart.

"But why? Are you arresting me?" May's voice wobbled in fear.

"Not at this stage."

"May, don't say anything. I'll get you a solicitor. This is madness." Lucy cried standing up.

Confused, May looked at Davey and asked, "Do I need a solicitor?"

"We're not arresting you, it's a formal interview," he repeated. "But you are considered a person of interest in the death of Josie Mathers."

"I can't afford a solicitor," May said in a small voice, now terrified.

" May, I'm going to call my solicitor. Don't say anything until he arrives." Lucy said.

There was no time to say more as the female constable took May's arm and walked her towards the house. When they arrived outside the back entrance to the hotel May was just in time to see Mary being put in the back of a police car, an officer's hand on her head, like you see on tv.

Knitting Socks in Sections

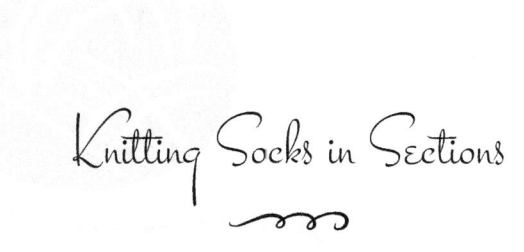

May didn't know how long she had been sitting waiting but it felt like hours since she had been put in the smelly cell. Her stomach was rumbling telling her it was positive it had missed dinner. There was no window in the room, only the table and four chairs and a camera up on the corner of the wall facing her. She was beginning to feel a bit panicky as she had needed the toilet for the past hour, she wished she hadn't had that extra cup of tea this afternoon. Luckily just when she thought she couldn't hold on any longer the door opened and DI Carley and DS Perrot as she must now think of him entered the room.

She stood up. "I'm desperate for the loo."

D I Carley spoke first, "Of course, Perrott get someone to take her."

Davey left the room, returning a few minutes later with a female officer.

When she returned to the room, she was cross and embarrassed.

Davey could see the sparks in her eyes and kept his fingers crossed that she wouldn't rile his boss who wasn't in the best of moods.

After all the preliminary official stuff was out of the way, Carley said.

"Let's go back to this argument you had with Josie, tell me again what happened?"

May remembered that Lucy had told her not to say anything but as she had already told Davey about the argument she thought it was okay to tell them again.

"So you were really angry. You were defending your friends. You don't like bullies. Had you had enough? Did you snap and kill her?" DI Carley asked.

"No!" May cried. "I would never hurt anyone."

"Didn't you predict, " he looked down at his notes, "that Josie would be found dead in the grotto murdered with a knitting needle?"

The blood seeped from May's face. As white as a sheet she swayed in her seat and Davey jumped up steadying her then turned her chair and pushed her head down between her knees.

When she felt better and was upright in her chair, DI Carley pushed a bottle of water across the table to her. She took a few gulps and then poured some in the cup of her hand, wiping it over her face and on the back of her neck. How did they know she said that about Josie? One of her so-called friends must have told them even though they'd promised not to. But thinking about it she couldn't blame them, it's not easy lying to the police and she shouldn't have asked them to.

"Are you ok to continue May?" Davey asked. He couldn't hide his concern and May took hope from that but the feeling didn't last long.

"You also told Josie that she would die alone. Tell us how you managed to get Josie to meet you in the grotto," Carley asked.

"No comment."

"Had you met Josie before this week?"

"No Comment."

"What did you do with your bloody clothes?"

"No comment."

"Okay Ms Wood, that's enough for now."

"Can I go now?" May asked.

"Oh no, we'll remove you to the cells until you decide to talk to us."

"But you said this was only an interview and I could leave whenever I wanted." Josie protested.

"I changed my mind."

With that D I Carley snapped the file shut, stood up and left the room, followed by DS Perrott.

What happened next was all a bit of a blur to May, she was taken down to be signed in. Her bag was taken, her jewellery, the laces from her trainers and her phone. Then she was taken to the cells by a cheerful policewoman. "There you go m'dear, cell number three, not exactly Saunton Sands Hotel but it's all inclusive."

The cell door made a resounding bang, the little flap went up and down and then she was on her own. It was all very surreal, one minute she was on a luxury break, the next she's in a police cell. How did that happen? What were her parents going to say? The smell, a mixture of stale body odour, food and urine, made her nauseous. Looking around the narrow room, there wasn't much to see. A low metal bed fixed to the wall with a rough cover and in the corner, horror of horrors, an open toilet. Thank God she went before coming in here. She vowed not to eat or drink anything whilst she was in here so that she didn't have to perform on that thing whilst being watched from the camera on the ceiling. Someone in a neighbouring cell was singing off key, the chorus of 'I will Always Love You', over and over. Using her trainer she worked the blanket off the bed and onto the floor, she would rather be cold than have that thing over her. No chance of that though because it was like an oven in the cell with no window to let air in. Exhausted, emotionally drained and hungry she sat hunched on the edge of the bed and let her tears fall. Wiping her face with the bottom of her t-shirt for the second time, she felt better for a good cry. I wonder what the time is? Can I work it out, it might help to pass the time. There's a joke there but sadly there's no one to share it with. It must be late. I'm hungry and I'm tired, I must have missed dinner. This has got to be a mistake, they'll realise in a minute. Davey will persuade that horrible inspector that I'm innocent. The only thing I'm guilty of killing is flies. Perhaps I need to stop that, could this be karma?

Casting On Various Methods

"Wake up m'dear," A hand jiggled her shoulder.

"Where am I?" May sat up

"Barnstaple Hilton, otherwise known as the Barnstaple nick. Come on, I've heard a rumour there's a nice cup of tea waiting." The policewoman took her by the elbow and helped her up.

"Oh thank you I'm dying for a cup of tea, is there any chance of a biscuit?"

"Oh, the tea is for me darlin and I'm off biscuits, I'm watching my weight." She grinned at May. Who wasn't sure if she was joking or not.

When she entered the interview room for the second time a distinguished looking man, dark hair, greying at the temples, a tall hawkish nose but kindly blue eyes and wearing a bespoke suit, rose from his chair and came to meet her. "Hello May, my name is Matthew Lock and I'm here to represent you. Come and sit down and we'll have a chat. Tea is on the way, I expect you could do with a cup." He pulled out a chair for her and she sat confused but heartily relieved to see that Carley and Davey weren't there. She'd thought they had brought her here to be questioned again.

She was a little bemused by the appearance of this man who was kind but exuded authority and confidence. All the duty solicitors she'd seen in tv dramas were either young and inexperienced or older, scruffy and jaded. Mr Lock was anything but. "Are you the duty solicitor Mr Lock, they must be paying you well?" The words were out of her mouth before she could stop them, she felt hot with embarrassment.

Before he could reply a constable knocked and entered carrying a tray with two mugs of tea and a plate of digestive biscuits. He placed them on the table and left without speaking.

May eyed the biscuits up hungrily but first she wanted to apologise for her outburst. It was only because she was scared, hungry and tired she wouldn't dream of saying anything like that normally.

He smiled at her. "You must be starving, help yourself. When you've sated your appetite a little we'll talk and please, call me Matthew." He leaned back in his chair quite relaxed.

May didn't need telling twice she picked up a biscuit in each hand and took alternate bites. Most people frightened and in unfamiliar surroundings couldn't eat but it hadn't quenched May's appetite it had the opposite effect. She sneaked a look at the solicitor, he looked expensive, that suit and those shoes were probably the equivalent to her annual wage. How did he manage to look so completely out of place but totally relaxed? She was still staring at him when he moved to push the empty plate away from her and pushed her mug of tea closer. When she looked at the plate she was surprised to see she'd eaten all the biscuits. She hastily brushed the crumbs off her now creased and grubby tee-shirt and denim shorts and took a sip of tea. It tasted like dishwater but it was hot and wet and provided a little comfort.

"To answer your earlier question, May, I am not the duty solicitor. Your friend Lucy instructed me."

"Wow, what a sweetheart. That's really lovely of her and I'm really grateful but I'm sorry she called you out Mr Lock because I think you are way out of my league. I'm a lowly teaching assistant and don't earn enough to even buy your suit. I can't afford to pay you and I don't think there is legal aid anymore. Of course I expect I'll have to pay for your call out fee and I bet it's more than a plumbers and they charge a bomb but..."

Matthew interrupted her. "It's Matthew and it's all taken care of May. Please don't worry about it for now. Let's concentrate on getting you out of here. I've read through your statements and looked at the evidence the police have. I can see nothing there that makes you a person of interest. You are no more a suspect than the other guests staying at the hotel where the murder occurred. Yes you found the body but you have no connection to the deceased or a motive. When the detectives come back to question you. I will speak for you if you must speak then answer with 'no comment'. Unless they are going to arrest you we will soon have you out of here in a jiffy."

"Really? I won't have to go back into the cells?" May couldn't help the wobble in her voice or the tears.

Matthew patted her on her arm. "You shouldn't have been in there in the first place. Chin up my dear." He walked over and opened the door, speaking a few words to the female constable standing outside. After about five minutes the door opened and DI Carley and DS Davey entered, May didn't look at them, keeping her eyes down.

There was silence for a few moments as Carley opened a buff coloured file he'd brought in with him and shuffled a few of the papers.

"Good morning sir, I'm Detective Inspector Carley and this is Detective Sergeant Perrot."

Matthew only responded with a nod at the two detectives, he didn't introduce himself, they knew who he was.

Davey after one quick look at May matched her, keeping his head down whilst Carley was speaking. He had been stunned when Carley walked away from her last interview and put her in the cells. Whatever Carley said he knew in his gut that May was innocent. After all she had been the one to tell them about the glass and decanter going missing, why would she do that if she was guilty. Once they knew about the glass and decanter it was highly likely poisoning was a possibility. However it was still a bit of a surprise to both of the detectives when the pathologist after doing a specialised test confirmed that the Colonel had indeed been poisoned.

"Why did you feel you needed a solicitor May, you are only here to answer a few questions we haven't arrested you?" Carley said.

"Why did you throw me in a cell then? I've never been in trouble in my whole life, I couldn't do my job working with children if I had." May said, cross that her voice was still a bit wobbly.

Matthew squeezed her arm again in warning. "May."

"We have a few more questions May." Carley said.

"Tell us why you threatened Josie? Was there another reason that you wanted her dead?"

"I didn't..."

Matthew put a restraining hand on May's arm and interrupted her. "Inspector, I have looked at your file and the statements Ms Wood has provided you with. There is nothing in your file that indicates Ms Wood is implicated in Josie Mathers death."

Before he could say any more Carley spoke. "New evidence has just come to light regarding Colonel Jeffries death. We think it's possible Josie Mathers witnessed the murder of the Colonel and that she was murdered to stop her speaking out. Ms Wood attacked the Colonel one evening giving him a nose bleed, she also had fights with Josie Mathers." He handed over some papers to the solicitor but didn't give him time to read them before continuing with his questioning. "Have you always had a violent temper, May?"

Matthew squeezed her arm again, warning her. May finally understood his silent messages.

"No comment."

"Inspector, this new information has nothing to do with my client. I object to your line of questioning."

Carley looked pointedly at Davey.

Davey forced a neutral expression and looked up at May. "You love gardens, don't you May?"

"No comment?" She replied but was confused by the question.

"Do you know a lot about plants May?" Davey asked.

"Inspector, are these questions relevant?" Matthew asked in a bored manner.

Davey carried on. "I'll ask you again. Do you know a lot about plants?"

May looked at Davey, "No."

Davey hated himself for what they were doing to May. It took all his strength to look at her without showing his emotions. He knew Carley had his reasons for suspecting her but he knew in his gut she wasn't capable of it. "But you do know about Aconite don't you and Aconite poisoning?".

"Okay detectives, that's enough. You're fishing, you have absolutely no evidence that points to my client. Ms Wood has given you a statement both at the time of the Colonel's death and at the death of Josie Mathers. So unless you are going to arrest her we are leaving. Come along May." Matthew stood up and helped May rise to her feet. Her legs were wobbly with exhaustion and she was glad of Matthew's strong supporting arm. She hesitated sure the detectives wouldn't let her go but with Matthew's arm supporting her, his confidence gave her hope.

Carley was livid but knew he had been outwitted. "DS Perrott will show you out. You are still a person of interest in our investigation Ms Wood and we may need to question you further." He snatched up his file, shoved his chair back with a screech and stormed out of the door.

. . .

The two detectives stood at the window in Carley's office and watched May step out of the lit vestibule with her solicitor.

"Sir Matthew Bloody Lock QC. How on earth did she manage to instruct such an eminent QC? Let alone get him here at three am in the morning." Carley asked.

Davey didn't answer, guessing it was a rhetorical question. Anyway he had no idea but he was pleased for May that she had someone so experienced to defend her.

"Sir, I meant to tell you earlier, they've identified the steel knitting needles used in Josie Mather's murder as being from the 1960's. They weren't new so that means one of the knitters must have brought them with them. I'll ring the woman who runs the knitting sessions in the morning and ask her which of the guests were experienced and might have brought them."

"Worth a try but I'm not sure that will point the finger at anybody. My wife inherited her mother's workbasket. It's not a basket but more a wooden box on legs, an antique piece. It contains sewing and knitting paraphernalia but my wife can't knit or sew a stitch. I had a bit of a rummage around in there and I found several sets of those steel double pointed needles. My point is anybody could have some. I would have been more excited if you had told me they'd found fingerprints on them." Carley said.

"I was just coming to that sir, they have found a partial thumb print on one of the needles."

"Why the hell didn't you say so instead prattling on about the 1960's? This is the break we needed, get the fingerprint people at the hotel first thing. And take everyone's prints including the cat if need be." Carley shouted the last sentence over his shoulder as he left.

Davey's shoulders slumped, his boss had interrupted him before he could go on to explain that the partial fingerprint was only a sliver and it was doubtful it could be used to identify the killer. He knew it would come back to bite him on the proverbial.

Dutch Heel

May was the first to arrive in the dining room on Friday morning. She was absolutely starving and had already eaten a banana but it wasn't long before the others joined her. As soon as May saw Lucy she jumped up and ran to her, flinging her arms around her and squeezing tight. "Lucy, thank you so much for saving me. I thought I was going to be stuck in that awful place. I don't know how I'm ever going to repay you but I will."

"May, you don't have to repay me. It's all taken care of.

Over Lucy's shoulder May saw Mary enter the dining room. She rushed to Mary, holding on to her upper arms. "Mary, are you ok? Did they put you in the cells like me? How did you get out?"

"Half a mo May, give the poor woman a chance and we all want to know what happened to you both. So let's sit down, have a cup of tea and you can both tell us your stories." Whilst Tony was talking he shepherded the two women back to the breakfast table pulling out two adjacent chairs for them to sit on then ran around to the opposite side.

May patted the seat the other side of her for Lucy then spoke. "Tony, I'm sorry to ask but I'm starving. I missed my dinner last night and only had a couple of biscuits at the police station. Would you mind fetching me a bowl of rice Krispies?"

Tony jumped up and filled two bowls with cereal, placing them in front of the two women and pushed the milk jug closer to May. She poured on a generous amount of milk then passed it to Mary who did the same. After eating a few mouthfuls, she started to speak but was interrupted by Jazz coming in.

"Oh! You're both back." She stopped just inside the door with a look of surprise fixed on her face.

May looked at her, "why are you so surprised Jazz? Surely you couldn't believe that Mary or I could have killed Josie?"

"No, well, I.. of course not but when the police took you away I thought." She tailed off.

"May and Mary are innocent. Have you come to take our breakfast orders?" Tony asked annoyed that Jazz could have thought his friends were murderers.

"Yes." Jazz replied.

"Then I suggest you do that and head back to the kitchen." Tony said firmly.

"He's so masterful," Michael said softly.

Jazz looked flustered for a moment but pulled herself together and held her notebook and pencil ready.

May spoke first. "I'll have a full English with extra sausage and extra bacon, two eggs, extra everything."

The others all gave their orders and Jazz left, Evelyn moved to close the door behind Jazz as she was closest.

May went on to recount everything that had happened to her and then turned to Mary. "Did Mr Lock get you out as well Mary?"

"No, I used my one phone call to call one of my sons and they sent a solicitor, I think I must have left a little after you did May, about twenty past three this morning."

"Uncle Matthew would have acted for you too Mary.

"Uncle Matthew?" May asked.

"Yes Sir Matthew Lock QC is my uncle and also my Godfather."

"Wow, how lucky am I to have you as a friend Lucy?"

The dining room door opened and over the next few minutes Walters and Jazz brought in the cooked breakfasts. Knowing it was the last day they could enjoy the luxury of having breakfast cooked for them, they had all ordered one.

Michael waited until the door was closed before he picked up the conversation. "So you are both in the clear, thank goodness we've been so worried. How horrible to have been put in a police cell, makes me shudder to think of it." Michael said.

"I don't know about you Mary but according to that Inspector Carley, I'm still on their suspect list as a person of interest." May said.

"Yes, me too. It's ridiculous, if I'd wanted to kill my sister over our inheritance why would I wait until we're staying here surrounded by lots of people. I could have popped her off easier at home." Mary replied.

"Has anyone seen Ursula this morning? I would have thought that her and Walters would be considered more likely suspects in the Colonel's murder." May said then stuffed a large piece of sausage in her mouth, closing her eyes with pleasure. "This breakfast is the food of the Gods. That Nancy can certainly cook."

"Clearly you nor Mary could have killed the Colonel or Josie, so who did?" May asked when she'd swallowed her sausage.

"Why don't we play detective and see what we can come up with?" Evelyn suggested.

"Ooh, I love a good murder mystery." Tony agreed.

"I hope the police find the murderer before they decide to come and take me away again." Mary shuddered. "I'm in. Let's meet up after breakfast on the terrace."

"Bring paper and pens so we can make notes," Lucy suggested.

"I'm bringing my knitting because I want to have my sock ready to finish this afternoon. I wish I'd had it with me whilst I was rotting in their stinky cell but then I suppose they would have taken the needles off me. They took everything, even the laces from my trainers." May said, "Shall we meet at ten, that gives us time to freshen up and fetch our knitting?"

Everyone agreed and they all left to go to their rooms. They were stopped at the door by Ursula, Walters, Jazz and Nancy and two police officers.

May's heart sank as she thought they had come for her again and was greatly relieved when it turned out that they had come to take everyone's fingerprints and DNA. By the time the police were finished and they were allowed to leave and been up to their rooms to fetch their knitting they were much later than intended when they all met on the terrace.

Joining Wool

"Do you mind if I don't write anything down, I'm still feeling a bit unsettled. I need to knit to restore my equilibrium." May said.

"No of course not, I'm happy to take notes as I am well ahead with my sock. I was so worried about you and Mary last night that after dinner I spent the rest of the evening in my room knitting. I'm ready to decrease for my toe, so I put that down and cast on for my second sock on the new pair of circular bamboo needles I bought from Ivy." Lucy said, turning over to a blank page in her notebook.

"Which do you like best, the steel or the bamboo?" Michael asked.

"I'm not really sure yet." Lucy replied. "I need to knit a bit more before I decide."

"Get with the programme people. I'm about to be arrested here for a murder I didn't commit can we concentrate please?"

"Yes, sorry May. Let's start with a list of suspects then we can look at them individually." Lucy said.

"Okay, are we going to include ourselves?" May asked.

They all looked at each other then May burst out laughing. "Let's assume that it's not one of us for the time being and concentrate on who is left. But if it turns out to be one of you I'll,"

Lucy interrupted her, "Don't say it May, that's what got you into trouble before."

"Okay Ms Bossy Librarian, you're probably right." May sighed at the realisation she really needed to be careful what she said until this nightmare was over. Her phone pinged. Ever since news of the murder had come out her parents and Trudy had been calling and texting her constantly wanting her to come home. She turned her phone on silent.

Lucy started writing. "Right, let's start our list with Ursula Jeffries, joint owner of Merton Manor. Walters, has he got another name?" No one knew so she carried on. "Walters, general factotum. Nancy, the Cook and Jazz, chambermaid and waitress. I won't include the gardeners, even the police weren't interested in them. It doesn't matter that we don't know the people on this list's full names, we know who we mean."

"Let's start with Ursula. She was having an affair. She didn't like her husband. She needed money and there might have been a big insurance pay out. And she had the means to poison him." May said, ticking off each statement on her fingers.

"Hang on, hang on, who said the Colonel was murdered?" Tony asked.

"Poison?" Michael asked.

"Oh, sorry, didn't I mention that? After they accused me of murdering Josie the police said that the Colonel had been poisoned and they thought I had done it and then killed Josie because she saw me, or something like that." May explained.

Everybody started talking at once and Lucy put her fingers to her lips and produced one of her piercing whistles.

May pulled a ball of yarn from her knitting bag and placed it on the table, keeping her hand on top. "We'll never get anywhere if we all talk at once. Let's try this. It's something I do with my students except obviously I don't use wool. Whoever has the ball of yarn can speak, then we won't be shouting over the top of each other." May held up the ball of yarn. "All I know is the Colonel was poisoned, I think with Aconite.

Lucy took the ball of yarn from her. "Is that what the police told you May.?" She handed the yarn back to May.

"They didn't tell me as such but they asked me if I knew about Aconite. I don't know one plant for another except for the more popular roses and tulips etc. But I googled it as soon as I got back here from the police station and it's incredibly toxic. Aconitum Napellus or Monkshood. It's a very pretty purple flower and it's quite possible there is some growing here in the gardens and if so then everyone has access to it." May replied.

"Let's get back to our list. Walters is next," Lucy suggested.

Michael picked up the ball of yarn. "Walters is in love with Ursula so he had a motive to get rid of the Colonel." Michael said. "I did try and find out a bit more about him but he has no social media presence and I couldn't find anything else."

"Now that the Colonel is out of the way he can marry Ursula and this place would be half his." Hazel said. "Oops sorry, forgot the yarn ball.

"They could have planned it together," Sheila said.

"That's a good point Hazel, working together to get rid of the Colonel." Tony agreed.

"Okay, let's move onto Nancy. She really loved the Colonel so I can't see her murdering him. Plus she thought he was going to marry her and they were going to make a success of this place, she also had ambitions for a michelin star" Lucy said.

"Yes but don't forget that Jazz told us they had had an enormous row when she threatened to tell Ursula about them. He humiliated her. He told her that he had women far prettier than her and that he'd had no intention of ever marrying her; he had only been stringing her along." May said

"That's definitely a strong motive. A woman scorned and all that." Michael said.

"How did they manage to get the poison into him anyway? I should imagine Aconite, like most poisons, tastes horrible." Tony said.

"Nancy is the one who has the best opportunity to poison him. She uses herbs from the garden. She prepares and cooks all the food and could probably disguise the taste with herbs and spices." May said.

"There is someone else who had access to the food preparation and cooking, the next on our list, Jazz."

"Oh come on Lucy that's a bit of a stretch. She's such a lovely girl and really caring." Evelyn said.

"I agree. She's young and pretty and could be out there enjoying herself or going to University or college to get a better job than this." Alice said.

"She's certainly bright enough. Instead, she's twenty four seven looking after her nan. We can definitely cross her off the list." Evelyn said.

"Plus she doesn't have a motive to kill either of them. I'm sure the Colonel was handsy with her but she was wise enough to keep out of his way. As for the way Josie treated her, she could easily get her own back by spitting in her dinner or serving her last, which she did." Michael said. "Well obviously I don't know if she did spit in her dinner but murder is a bit extreme."

"I've had a lot of time to think about this whilst I was sitting in that stinky cell."

Lucy gave her hand a squeeze in sympathy.

May smiled her thanks and carried on. "I think the poison must have been in the Colonel's Whisky. The glass and the decanter were definitely there when I found Nancy with the Colonel's body at about twenty past seven in the morning, I told the police that in my statement."

"I remember seeing the decanter first thing too and when I

was interviewed I told DS Flower but I didn't remember seeing the glass." Tony said."

"The Colonel certainly had a fair bit to drink that evening. He was drinking whisky before dinner then there was wine at the dinner table and we took all the bottles out to finish on the terrace, so we were all drinking that. He must have had more whisky after we had all left the terrace. Perhaps he was so tiddly that he drank it straight down before he realised there was something wrong with it," suggested Lucy.

"Good thinking Lucy, that's probably it, I think you could be right. So who had access to the whisky decanter?" May asked.

"That's a big problem, because we all did. We were all in and out of the sitting room where the bar is." Tony said.

"No, sorry Tony but you're wrong there. The whisky from the bar came out of a bottle but the decanter that I saw must have been the Colonel's own personal one and he probably kept it in his study. Didn't you notice the Georgian silver whisky label on it? That on its own is probably worth about a hundred and fifty quid let alone the decanter and what he was drinking from the bar earlier was the cheap stuff." May said.

"Well that narrows it down to three people, Ursula, Walters and Nancy." Lucy said.

"I'm not sure we should discount Jazz, Hercule Poroit wouldn't." May grinned.

"True, I'll leave her on the list. How are we going to find out which one it is then because let's be honest we're not Hercule Poroit or Miss Marple even if we knit like her." Lucy laughed.

"I've been thinking about that too. I think we should set a trap." May said.

A lot of excited chatter broke out and Lucy once again whistled to bring everyone to order.

"What happened to only speaking if you have the ball of yarn?" Lucy asked, looking around at them sternly.

"Ooh you've got your stern librarian face on." Tony said.

May grabbed for the ball of yarn. "Hear me out before you all object. The police are stuck at the moment. They are concentrating on me and Mary as being the most likely suspects and I don't think they are even looking at anyone else. I don't know about you Mary but I'm not going to sit around doing nothing but wait to be arrested."

"I don't think you are giving the police enough credit to be honest May. All three of those detectives strike me as being very competent and I don't think we should be putting ourselves in danger by playing detectives ourselves." Lucy said.

"I agree, it's one thing, writing a suspect list and chewing it over between us but it's quite another actually going after the killer." Mary said.

The others all agreed.

"Well I'm not asking all of you to put yourselves at risk. It's going to be me and I'm warning you all now, you will not be able to change my mind, so why don't you all listen to my plan first?" May sat back whilst they all argued amongst themselves. When they were quiet again May told them her plan.

"We have only got what's left of this morning and lunch time because we all want to do the workshop later and finish our sock. Then it's time to go home, so this is what I propose. I'm guessing that Ursula will join us for lunch as it's the last meal we'll have here."

"There is the cream tea later." Tony said.

"Yes but I think it's more likely she will join us for lunch and leave the cream tea to Ivy. Walters and Jazz will be serving lunch and we could ask Ursula if Nancy could come out from the kitchen and share coffee with us so we can thank her for all her lovely meals during our stay. When we are all relaxed and drinking our coffee I'm going to have an epiphany,"

"Bless you," Tony said.

"Ha ha, very funny. I'm going to say that I have only just realised that something I saw may help the police identify the killer. I'm going to leave the table saying I'm going back to the grotto to get it sorted in my head and then when I've thought it through I'll ring Inspector Carley. If you all get up and say you are going to your rooms to pack before coming down for the last workshop the killer will think they have the perfect opportunity to stop me." May put the yarn ball down, leaned back in her chair and picked up her sock knitting, looking pleased with herself.

"No. Way. That is absolute madness, if the police are right and this person killed both the Colonel and Josie they are extremely dangerous and probably won't hesitate to kill again to save their own skin." Lucy said.

"Great plan May for the murderer. What on earth makes you think you

can defend yourself against this person?" Tony was angry.

"You know we are not going to let you do this don't you? And you can't do it without our cooperation." Michael said.

"Michael's right, we won't help you with this madcap idea." Lucy said, folding her arms. The others all agreed but May put her hand up to stop them speaking.

"Give me a bit of credit here you woolly wonders. I'm not going to be on my own. I'm not that stupid. You lot won't be going to your rooms to pack your bags, you'll just pretend. I don't know if any of you have noticed but if you walk around the main upstairs landing and then go down the hallway, at the end is a narrow hidden door. It opens on to a secret staircase that goes up to the servants quarters and down to the ground floor. At the bottom there is one door leading to the outside and another to the kitchen; it must have been used by the servants when they weren't meant to be seen by the posh knobs. It might still be used for all I know but it is ideal for our plan." May said.

"Oh it's our plan now is it?" Lucy said, frowning at her.

"Yes, it is." May smiled. "If you all go to your rooms after lunch, the killer will think I'm all alone in the garden. But I won't be alone because you lot will use the hidden staircase to get out into the garden without being seen. Not all at once, we don't want anyone in the kitchen to hear you, we don't want a stampede ." She chuckled."

"I don't know how you can laugh when you are setting yourself up as bait." Alice said.

May ignored the remark and carried on. "I'm going to make my way to the grotto but don't worry I'm not going in. I don't think I'll ever want to go in there again but its location is ideal. If you can secrete yourselves about the garden, not near the terrace because that is the way I think our killer will come. Then gradually form a hidden circle around the grotto area and wait. When the killer arrives and reveals themselves I'll say their name really loudly and then you can all move in. Job done." May said smugly.

"What if the killer creeps up on you and doesn't give you time to say their name? I don't like it. It's too dangerous." Lucy said, biting her lip.

"I'll stand with my back to the wall of the entrance but anyway I'll see them coming along the path when they get close enough." May assure her. "There are seven of you, eight including me against one of them. And we're armed with Lucy's whistle.

There was silence for a few moments as they all thought about May's mad suggestion.

"You are going to do it anyway, even without our help aren't you?" Lucy asked.

"Yep."

"As much as I hate it, I'm going to help you." Lucy said.

The others, one after the other like a row of dominoes, fell into place agreeing to help.

"I'm not a very fast runner though May." Evelyn said.

"Don't worry Evelyn you don't need to be. The idea is that we will all surround them and be able to identify the killer, whoever it is can't kill all of us." May chuckled.

"Well that's not exactly true is it? They could May ." Tony said.

"Thanks Tony, not helping. Look I don't think this person wants to kill again, they're not likely to have a gun or anything and they won't be catching us by surprise like they did Josie. Once we've identified them we can let them escape. You can all have your fingers poised to dial 999, we'll let the police deal with them." May assured them.

"So we are not trying to catch them ourselves then?" Sheila asked.

"No. so let's all relax, do a bit of knitting and try not to think about it until lunchtime, okay?" May asked.

Shaping Legs Of Socks

They were all sitting in the dining room waiting for their lunch, May kept nervously glancing at the door. They really needed Ursula to join them for lunch for their plan to go ahead. There was a place laid for her so she felt hopeful. The door opened but it was only Walters. He stepped back for Ursula to enter then moved to the table and held her chair out.

Ursula looked strained and tired, she smiled around at the group. "Good afternoon everyone. When I started this venture I certainly didn't expect the catastrophic events that you have had to endure this week. I only wish I could say that this week has been the most relaxing retreat. But I sincerely hope that you have managed to at least enjoy the comfort of your rooms, the good food, the excursions and most of all the excellent sock knitting workshops run by our expert Ivy. As a gesture of our goodwill, I will be offering you a generous discount on any further knitting workshops you might like to attend."

Whilst she was talking, Walters had been pouring some sparkling wine in everyone's glasses. He then held his own glass up and spoke. "This is a non alcoholic sparkling wine, I hope you will all join me in a toast to our hostess, Ursula."

May looked around at the others, they looked as surprised as she was but they held their glasses up and toasted their hostess, who didn't look that pleased about it.

"That's enough Walters, go and help Jazz serve lunch."

He looked daggers at her for a second then swept out of the door.

They all enjoyed their lunch of a deconstructed prawn cocktail , followed by a lemon herb chicken and salad. Nancy proudly carried the desert in and it looked splendid, a layered strawberry mousse cake. The almond sponge cake base was topped with strawberry mousse and had a circle of halved strawberries around the outside. Then another almond sponge cake on top, decorated with more halved strawberries and piped cream. It was a work of art and they all oohed and aahed eager to try it.

"Nancy, that looks wonderful." May said.

Nancy brought out a decorated cake slice from her jacket pocket but May stopped her. "Can I take a picture of it first Nancy?"

Nancy stepped back whilst May took her picture. "I can put it on our Sock-Chat group if any of you want."

Whilst May was serving the cake May took the opportunity to speak. "Ursula, would you mind if Nancy joined us for coffee. We would like to thank her for feeding us so well."

Ursula didn't look at Nancy but agreed. "Nancy is welcome to stay, Jazz and Walters can manage the coffee. Take a seat when you've finished serving Nancy."

Nancy sat down in a chair as far away from Ursula as possible. May waited until Jazz and Walters were in the room and serving the last coffee. "Do you know something has just popped into my head, how strange, something about Josie's murder. I didn't even think about it at the time but now I've had time to mull it over I realise it could be really important. Will you excuse me? I'm going out to the Grotto to check something and get my thoughts in order then I'll ring Inspector Carley. I'll meet you all later on the terrace ready for this afternoon's workshop." She gulped down the last of her coffee and left the dining room.

Unexplained Knots

May leant against the wall of the grotto, she was beginning to wish she had listened to the others and that she hadn't eaten so much lunch. Her stomach was going up and down like a lift on steroids. She was getting whiplash from turning her head from side to side checking to see if someone was coming. How could she have forgotten that you can't see who is coming from the other side of the grotto because that side of the path bends around the grotto sharply. She had to hope that the killer, whoever they were, would soon turn up, the suspense was killing her. Oops, wrong choice of words, she thought smiling but her smile soon slipped when she heard footsteps crunching along the stony path.

"You! Oh faggots. But you aren't even on our suspect list. How on earth could we have forgotten you?" May's mind was working at warp speed. She stepped away from the Grotto wall and out onto the path. She hadn't seen Ryder since the morning she discovered the body and she hadn't thought about him for a minute. She'd been too busy coping with being taken to the police station and held in a cell. How could they all have forgotten him? Damn and blast, although he was a bit of a poser she had quite fancied him but obviously not enough to remember him. She only hoped the others were in position around them both. She shouted his name, "Ryder! I never suspected you for a minute."

Surprised, he walked closer to her. "What's up May?"

"Don't come any closer Ryder." Terrified, she shouted his name again and put her hands out as if to halt him. Where the hell are the others? I don't want to die, she thought and her face crumpled as tears sprang to her eyes. Still he came for her.

Seemingly out of nowhere Jazz appeared behind Rider and whacked him over the head with a garden spade. He was so close to May that as he went down his head caught the side of May's temple and she went down, the back of her head hitting the path with a dull thud. By the time she swam back into consciousness she didn't realise that she had been moved. Now she was lying across the path, face down close to the rock pool. Her head was pounding, she didn't know what bit hurt worse, the back of her head or the side. Groggily she managed to push herself up on her hands and slowly turned her head. She saw Jazz standing over Ryder, the spade raised up behind her shoulder. "Oh thank God you came Jazz, you saved my life. Ryder is the murderer. Call the police."

Jazz moved away from Ryder who was still unconscious to stand next to her with the spade still in her hands. "Oh dear, poor May. You think you are so clever but you are in fact really stupid."

May was confused, she looked up at Jazz, her eyes were cold and flat, showing no emotion.

"Did you think I would fall for your little play acting at lunch? It was pathetic, so ridiculously obvious it was a trap."

May felt nauseous and weak but she knew she had to get to her feet if she was going to stand any chance of staying alive. Where were the others? Why hadn't come to help her? She tried to get to her knees but Jazz pushed her down with a Doc Martin clad foot on her back.

"It's not Ryder, it was you. You are the killer."

Jazz laughed and it didn't sound very sane to May who was

looking around desperately hoping her friends would arrive to save her.

"Looking for your little friends to come and rescue you? Forget it. As soon as they went up to their rooms, I locked them all in. You can forget about anybody else coming. Ursula and Walters are in her office arguing and Nancy is busy making scones for this afternoon's cream tea. What a shame you're going to miss it. Nancy makes the most delicious scones."

She's totally mad thought May. I am going to die.

Jazz carried on as if she was telling a story. "I heard you all on the terrace making your stupid plan to trap the murderer and how they were going to come to your rescue. You've made it so easy for me putting yourself here all alone in the very place that I had to get rid of that other stupid woman. And when the police arrive they'll find Ryder dead from a blow to the head and you sadly drowned in the rock pool. They'll assume he is the killer and that you challenged him. You both fought and you hit him with the spade and killed him. Sadly you passed out due to your injuries and your head slipped under the water. And you drowned"

May's heart sank, she's right, the police will think Ryder is the killer. They won't even look for anyone else, she'll get away with it. In books they always talk to the killer to buy time, it's my only hope. The others will know something's wrong when they find themselves locked in. They'll come for me.

"Why did you kill the Colonel Jazz? Was it because he tried to assault you? If that was the case then it would have been self-defence"

"Do you think I'd let that disgusting old man touch me? He tried it a few times. The last time he came into the kitchen to find Nancy. I was peeling the veg and he tried it on, I told him that if he ever laid a finger on me again, it would be for the last time. That he'd have no fingers left to touch any woman again. I think it helped that I had the razor sharp vegetable knife in my hand at the time."

"Good for you Jazz."

"Don't patronise me." Jazz lifted the spade.

"I wasn't, I promise. I was genuinely impressed with how you sorted him out. So why did you kill him then?"

"It was because of nan." Tears sprung to Jazz's eyes and she wiped them on her sleeve.

"What did he do to your nan?"

"My nan is the sweetest, kindest hard-working woman and she didn't deserve what he did to her."

"Tell me about it."

Jazz stood the spade on its end and leaned on the handle. "My Nan was the cook here, she worked for Ursula's dad then for Ursula for over forty years. When the Colonel married Ursula, he gave my Nan the sack and brought Nancy in. I know it's not Nancy's fault, nor Ursulas' she did try to keep Nan. That man was a controlling pig. He didn't even give Nan notice or pay, she was devastated. Ursula did give her some money a bit later because she felt so guilty about Nan but it wasn't just about the money. From that day on Nan gave up on life, she hasn't got out of her bed since. She barely eats and now her mind is going, the doctor said it's the stress and the shock. The Colonel might just have well of shot her because the day he sacked her she died. Nan brought me up, you know, gave me everything. I love her to bits.

That night before dinner, the Colonel caught me in the hallway and told me off for being late that morning and said if it happened again he'd have to let me go. I told him that Nan was sick and I had to look after her and if I was sometimes late or had to leave early I always made up the time. Nancy understood and didn't mind. Do you know what he said?"

"No."

"He said, tell the lazy bitch to get a job and let you do yours. I hated him. I could have killed him where he stood. Why should I let him live when Nan didn't have a reason to anymore?"

"What an awful thing to say. Your poor Nan and poor you.

He really was an appalling man. But why kill Josie? Was it because she was so nasty to you or did she see you do something?"

"I'm not really sure what she'd seen but she sent me a note saying that she had seen what I'd done and to meet her in the grotto. I wondered if she'd been in the garden and seen me pull up an Aconite plant. I wanted to find a plant that I could use to make him sick and pay him back for what he'd done to Nan. I looked it up, Aconite can't be detected by ordinary toxicology tests. So when he got sick if they did tests they wouldn't suspect poison. Josie knew Aconite was poisonous, she knows a lot about plants. She probably saw me when she was in the garden pinching bits of plants for cuttings. She'd been doing it all week, she had a load of them up in her room in a special container. She was always spying on everyone from her bedroom window and I didn't know if she'd seen me with the Colonel. I'd been really careful. I waited till everyone had gone to bed, Walters was the last to leave and he left the Colonel to lock up. I took out a bottle of his personal whisky on the pretence of topping up his decanter and I dropped the aconite in. He was so drunk he didn't notice but I thought I had only put in enough to make him sick. I couldn't believe it when I came in the next morning and he was dead. I tried to get the glass and the decanter to wash them out but they had already disappeared. I didn't mean to kill him and I was terrified that the police would suspect me but then they decided it was natural causes. It was brilliant, I was safe. It was such a relief."

"So what happened with Josie?"

"Well, it was the note that bitch sent me saying she knew what I had done and to meet her in the grotto unless I wanted her to tell the police. She obviously knew something I had to shut her up. It was her own fault. She had to die. You and Mary fighting with her after dinner gave me the perfect opportunity to frame you, so I told the police about you and Mary arguing with Josie. Then I used the knitting needles to kill her so that the police would think it was one of you knitters and it worked because they took you and Mary away."

Jazz had looked away from May as she started talking. Lost in her own story she was staring out over the garden and after a while took her foot off of May's back. May knew this might be her last and only chance to escape. Although still feeling a bit woolly in the head, she very slowly rose up onto her knees. It was the wrong move. Jazz flew at her and pushed her back down. May went down her forehead thudding into the path. She was only semi-conscious as Jazz, struggling with her dead weight dragged her closer to the rock pool. Eventually she managed it and May's head dropped down into the water. Jazz sat back on her heels and smiled, satisfied that the scene now looked how she wanted. Jazz, your work here is over, she thought. Now I only have to wait till I hear someone coming and pretend I'm trying to save May.

Davey had driven out to Merton Manor with Sonya; they were to search the garden for Aconite plants. They had split up and Davey, who was searching fairly near to the grotto heard voices and went to investigate. As he came around the back of the grotto he was astonished to see Jazz kneeling next to May whose head was hanging into the rock pool. "Hang on Jazz , I'm coming." He dropped to his knees on the other side of May and reaching for her waist managed to drag her head out of the rock pool. Jazz jumped up screaming with rage, she picked up the spade and flew at him, hitting him with the spade and knocking him backwards. Jazz dropped the spade and dragged May back towards the rock pool. Davey was dazed but still conscious. With blood running down his face he reached for Jazz and grabbed hold of her legs pulling her down. He tried to grab her wrists but she was wild and fought back, hitting him in the face over and over. He was trying to roll her over so he could get on top and use his weight to pin her down.

Ryder came too and pulled himself up to sit, the pain in his head made him groan and he desperately wanted to lay his head down but he saw Davey fighting Jazz. Supporting himself against the grotto wall he pulled himself upright and staggered towards them. He managed to grab Jazz around the waist and tried to pull her off Davey but Davey shouted at him, "May! She's in the rock pool quickly man, help her." Ryder turns and sees May, the top of her head partially submerged. Dragging her from the water he turned her on her back shouting at her, when she didn't respond he started to give her the kiss of life. Sonya arrived running from behind the grotto and soon made quick work of wrenching Jazz's arms behind her back and snapping on a pair of handcuffs. Jazz was still struggling and kicking so Tracy with a bit of difficulty fastened some plastic ties around her ankles pulling them tight and pushed her over onto her side on the path. Jazz wasn't going anywhere.

Although it had looked as if May's face was in the water, in fact it was only the top of her head up to her nose leaving her mouth free to breathe. She swam back to consciousness to find Ryder's mouth over her face. "Eugh!" She tried to shove him away. "Get off me."

Davey dropped down onto his knees on her other side." Move back, give her some space."

"You move back. I've got this." Ryder said.

"I'm a trained first aider and a police detective. I'm in charge here."

The two men leaned back on their heels and glowered at each other with May lying in the middle of them.

A thunder of footsteps heralded the arrival of the knitting gang, Tony in the lead.

"Oh fish on a bike! Whatever has happened? May are you alright?" Tony dropped to his knees next to Ryder and Michael dropped down next to Davey.

"Right, that's it. Enough. I feel like the Virgin Mary in the stable. Help me get up you idiots, you're certainly not wise men. And stop shouting, my head hurts."

Kitchener Stitch. (Herbert Kitchener, British Secretary of State for WW1 promoted the Kitchener stitch to be used for soldiers' socks to prevent chafing)

"Okay, so we all have fourteen stitches on our two needles except for Tony who has sixteen because of his big feet," Ivy chuckled as the others laughed. "Place your needles parallel together, the sewing needle and the yarn are coming from the back needle." Ivy then slowly went through the process until they were all chanting, knit on, purl off, purl off, knit on. Ivy was bobbing about between them checking that everybody was managing until Michael, the last to finish, laid his completed sock down.

"Give yourselves a round of applause. You are all now officially sock knitters." Ivy said, starting the clapping. "Despite everything that's been thrown at you this week you have still managed to carry on and complete your sock. An extra round of applause for May who has been an absolute heroine. She caught a killer, has a killer headache and still managed to complete her sock." She waited for the clapping to stop then spoke again. "It has been a difficult time for all of us these past couple of years. For me as a business this first workshop has been very important for me. If this workshop is successful then hopefully there will be many more. I hesitate in passing these feedback forms around, bearing in mind the extraordinary events of this week but if you wouldn't mind filling them in, I would appreciate it. I have also brought my sock yarn with me if anyone wants to take another look. Our cream tea will be here in about twenty minutes so there is plenty of time for a browse and a comfort break."

May started a round of applause and cheering which became slightly over the top and a bit hysterical. She had to put her fingers in her ears to block the noise out because of her headache. The medics had checked her over but she had refused to go to the hospital with Ryder who was being taken in because of his head injury. She had promised that if her headache persisted or she felt ill she would go straight to A & E.

After they had finished looking over Ivy's yarns and put their finished sock and yarns away they were all settled back in their chairs looking forward to afternoon tea.

Ursula, Walters and Nancy brought out cake stands with tiers of tiny finger sandwiches with the crusts cut off, mini quiches, puff pastry whirls with cheese and onion, a selection of small cakes of all description and large golden scones with dishes brimming with clotted cream and homemade jam. When they had delivered the teapots, milk, sugar and cups and saucers, they pulled up another table and joined their guests.

After everybody had tucked in Ursula spoke up. "Thank you all for being our first guests and despite the unexpected tragic events staying and seeing out the week. We hope that you will visit us again. In your rooms you will find a discount voucher for a further knitting retreat of your choice. Despite everything Ivy, our guests have given positive feedback and expressed their wish to return for further workshops, so thank you. Ivy beamed at this news. Ursula then remembered something, she stretched across the table to May holding out an envelope. "May, a certain detective sergeant left this for you."

The others all whooped and laughed as May took the envelope, blushing."

· · ·

The End

Afterword

Thank you dear reader for buying this book. I love knitting socks and I hope you will have a go, it's not as hard as you might think. My own family won't wear anything else. Please leave a review on Amazon if you can, it means so much to us authors.

The wonderful Debbie & Sam from Pick 'N' Stitch have provided this sock pattern designed by their mother Pat. They have my sincere thanks for giving me permission to print the pattern here for those of you who may have been inspired to make your own.

Knitting Pattern

The wonderful Debbie & Sam from Pick 'N' Stitch have provided this sock pattern designed by their mother Pat.

KNITTING PATTERN

Pick 'n' Stitch Ltd

Basic Sock Pattern

MATERIALS INCLUDED
Sock yarn - 1 ball of Funny Feetz 100g
Set of 3.25mm double pointed knitting needles

IMPORTANT
To ensure accuracy only the yarn supplied in this kit is suitable. No responsibility will be taken for the result of using any other yarn.

ABBREVIATIONS
K: Knit
Sl: slip
PSSO: Pass slipped stitch over
P: Purl
P2tog: purl 2 together
K2tog: Knit 2 together

Pick 'n' Stitch Ltd
4 Hertsfield Avenue, Rochester, Kent. ME2 3PU
Website : www.picknstitch.co.uk Email : picknstitch@btinternet.com
© This leaflet is protected by copyright. Reproduction in any form (including photocopy) is strictly forbidden. Offenders will be prosecuted.

KNITTING PATTERN

Pick 'n' Stitch Ltd

INSTRUCTIONS
Cast on 60 sts over 3 needles
Work rounds of K1 P1 rib for 6 cm
Continue in stocking stitch (each row knit as working in rounds) until work measures 14 cm from beginning, finishing at end of a round.

Divide for Heel
Knit 13, turn and slip last 14 sts of round on to the other end of this same needles (27sts)
Divide remaining 33 sts onto 2 needles and leave for instep.
Work backwards and forwards on heel sts in stocking stitch (one row knit, one row purl as now working back and forth and not in the round) for 8 cm, ending with a purl row.

Turn heel
Turn Heel

Now start to turn the heel on the 27 stitches that you have been working on

1st row: k17 sl1 k1 PSSO turn (26 stitches)
2nd row: sl1 P7 p2tog turn (25 stitches)
3rd row: sl1 K8 sl1 k1 PSSO turn (24 stitches)
4th row: sl1 P9 p2tog turn (23 stitches)
5th row: sl1 k10 sl1 k1 psso turn (22 stitches)
6th row: sl1 p11 p2tog turn (21 stitches)
7th row: sl1 k12 sl1 k1 psso turn (20 stitches)
8th row: sl1 p13 p2tog turn (19 stitches)
9th row: sl1 k14 sl1 k1 psso turn (18 stitches)
10th row: sl1 p15 p2tog turn (17 stitches)

Pick 'n' Stitch Ltd
4 Hertsfield Avenue, Rochester, Kent. ME2 3PU
Website : www.picknstitch.co.uk Email : picknstitch@btinternet.com
© This leaflet is protected by copyright. Reproduction in any form (including photocopy) is strictly forbidden. Offenders will be prosecuted.

KNITTING PATTERN

Pick 'n' Stitch Ltd

Slip the instep stitches back onto one needle

Knit 9 stitches from your original 17 stitches onto one needle
Knit 8 stitches from your original 17 stitches onto next needle, plus pick up and knit 21 stitches up the side of the heel flap
Knit across 33 stitches from the instep onto 3rd needle
Knit 21 stitches down the side of the heel flap and then knit your first 9 stitches again

This should then leave you with stitches over 3 needles as follows
29 stitches
33 stitches
30 stitches

If you have these split over 4 needles, then I would rearrange them so that they are now on 3 needles, in the proportions as shown above. Then when you start your decreasing below, you are effectively decreasing the stitches that you have picked up from the heel flap.

Next round knit
Next round
       1st needle – knit to last 2 stitches, k2tog
       2nd needle – knit all stitches
       3rd needle – sl1 k1 psso, knit to end

Pick 'n' Stitch Ltd
4 Hertsfield Avenue, Rochester, Kent. ME2 3PU
Website : www.picknstitch.co.uk Email : picknstitch@btinternet.com
© This leaflet is protected by copyright. Reproduction in any form (including photocopy) is strictly forbidden. Offenders will be prosecuted.

Pick 'n' Stitch Ltd

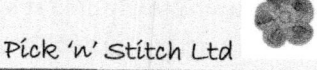

Repeat these 2 rounds (decreasing every alternate row) until you have 60 stitches in total which should be split as

- 1st needle = 13 stitches
- 2nd needle = 33 stitches
- 3rd needle = 14 stitches

Continue without shaping until work measures 19cm from back of heel or desired length, finishing at the end of a round.

Then

Slip 2 stitches from the second needle on to the first needle, and 1 stitch from the end of the second needle on to the third needle.

Ending up with

Needle 1 = 15 stitches
Needle 2 = 30 stitches
Needle 3 = 15 stitches

Shape Toe

On 1st needle [k to last 3 sts, k2tog, k1], on 2nd needle [k1 sl1, k1, psso, k to last 3 sts, k2tog, k1], on 3rd needle [k1, sl1, k1 psso, k to end]
Next round: k (4 decreases per alternate round)
Repeat last 2 rounds 10 times (20 rounds) until you have 20 stitches
Needle 1 = 5 stitches
Needle 2 = 10 stitches
Needle 3 = 5 stitches
then k sts from 1st needle onto 3rd needle and graft stitch

Pick 'n' Stitch Ltd
4 Hertsfield Avenue, Rochester, Kent. ME2 3PU
Website : www.picknstitch.co.uk Email : picknstitch@btinternet.com
© This leaflet is protected by copyright. Reproduction in any form (including photocopy) is strictly forbidden. Offenders will be prosecuted.

They have my sincere thanks for giving me permission to print the pattern here for those of you who may have been inspired to make your own.

Pick 'n' Stitch Ltd. All rights reserved to this sock knitting pattern. They are protected by copyright and are for personal use

KNITTING PATTERN

only and must not be made for resale or any commercial purposes.

No part of this sock pattern (including it's photography) may be reproduced, stored in a retrieval system or transmitted in any form or by any means without the prior permission in writing from Pick 'N' Stitch Ltd

Shop for sock kits, yarn and patterns at www.picknstitch.co.uk & PicknStitchUK (by Debbie and Sam) - Etsy UK

Acknowledgments

My thanks and love as always to my family. My dear husband Roger, for providing me with endless cups of tea when I'm writing and always being there for me. My wonderful children, their partners, my beloved grandchildren and my two furry companions Treacle & Winnie. I am so lucky to have them all in my life.

Enormous thanks to my two dear friends Terri E and Leigh C for being brave enough to read this book, point out my errors, tell me what doesn't work and for their support.

Special thanks as always to my son Adam, without him my books would never see the light of day. I am truly grateful for his time, his care, his expertise and his unwavering support.

Printed in Great Britain
by Amazon